Ice Cream

Helen Dunmore

LARGE PRINT
Oxford and Orlando

Copyright © Helen Dunmore, 2000

First published in Great Britain 2000
by Viking

Published in Large Print 2000 by ISIS Publishing Ltd,
7 Centremead, Osney Mead, Oxford OX2 0ES, and
ISIS Publishing, PO Box 195758,
Winter Springs, Florida 32719-5758, USA
by arrangement with Penguin Group

British Library Cataloguing in Publication Data
Dunmore, Helen, 1952-
  Ice cream. – Large print ed.
  1. Large type books
  I. Title
  823.9'14[F]

ISBN 0-7531-6325-X (hb)
ISBN 0-7531-6328-4 (pb)

Printed and bound by Antony Rowe, Chippenham and Reading

ICE CREAM

CONTENTS

My Polish Teacher's Tie

I wear a uniform, blue overall and white cap with the school logo on it. Part-time catering staff, that's me, £3.89 per hour. I dish out tea and buns to the teachers twice a day, and I shovel chips on to the kids' trays at dinner-time. It's not a bad job. I like the kids.

The teachers pay for their tea and buns. It's one of those schemes teachers are good at. So much into a kitty, and that entitles them to cups of tea and buns for the rest of the term. Visitors pay, too, or it wouldn't be fair. Very keen on fairness, we are, here.

It was ten-forty-five when the Head got up to speak. He sees his staff together for ten minutes once a week, and as usual he had a pile of papers in front of him. I never listen to any of it as a rule, but as I was tipping up the teapot to drain I heard him mention Poland.

I am half-Polish. They don't know that here. My name's not Polish or anything. It was my mother, she came here after the war. I spoke Polish till I was six, baby Polish full of rhymes Mum taught me. Then my father put a stop to it. "You'll get her all mixed up, now she's going to school. What use is Polish ever going to be to her?" I can't speak it now. I've got a tape, a tape of me speaking Polish with Mum. I listen, and I think I'm going to understand what we're saying, and then I don't.

1

". . . long-term aim is to arrange a teacher exchange — several Polish teachers are looking for penfriends in English schools, to improve their written English . . . so if you're interested, the information's all here . . ."

He smiled, wagging the papers, and raised his eyebrows. I wrung out a cloth and wiped my surfaces. I was thinking fast. Thirteen minutes before I was due downstairs.

The meeting broke up and the Head vanished in a knot of teachers wanting to talk to him. I lifted the counter-flap, tucked my hair under the cap, and walked across. Teachers are used to getting out of the way of catering staff without really seeing them.

"Excuse me," I said, pushing forward, "excuse me," and they did. Then I was in front of the Head. "Excuse me," I said again, and he broke off what he was saying. I saw him thinking, *trouble*. The kids chucking chips again. He stitched a nice smile on his face and said, "Oh, er — Mrs, er — Carter. Is there a problem?"

"No," I said, "I was just wondering, could I have that address?"

"Address?"

"The Polish one. You said there was a Polish teacher who wanted an English penfriend."

"Oh. Ah, yes. Of course." He paused, looking at me as if it might be a trick question. "Is it for yourself?"

"I'd like to write to a Polish teacher."

"Oh," he said. "Yes. Of course, Mrs Carter."

I took the address and smiled at him.

When Steve's first letter came I saw he'd taken it for granted I was a teacher. The person he had in his head when he was writing to me was an English teacher, a real professional. This person earned more money than him and had travelled and seen places and done things he'd never been able to do. He was really called Stefan, but he said he was going to call himself Steve when he wrote to me.

Jade saw the letter. "What's that, Mum?"

"Just a letter. You can have the stamp if you want."

In the second letter Steve told me that he wrote poetry. *"I have started a small literary magazine in our department. If you want, I am happy to send you some of our work."*

I told him about Jade. I told him about the songs my mother taught me in Polish, the ones I used to know but I'd forgotten. I didn't write anything about my job. Let him think what he wanted to think. I wasn't lying.

The first poem he sent me was about a bird in a coal mine. He sent me the English translation. This bird flew down the main shaft and got lost in the tunnels underground, then it sang and sang until it died. Everyone heard it singing, but no one could find it. I liked that poem. It made me think maybe I'd been missing something, because I hadn't read any poetry since I left school. I wrote back, *"Send me the Polish, just so I can see it."* When the Polish came I tried it over in my head. It sounded a bit like the rhymes my mother used to sing.

At first we wrote every week, then it was twice. I used to write a bit every day then make myself wait until the middle of the week to send it. I wrote after Jade was in bed. Things would suddenly come to me. I'd write, *"Oh,*

Steve, I've just remembered . . .", or *". . . Do you see what I mean, Steve, or does it sound funny?"* It made it seem more like talking to him when I used his name.

He wrote me another poem. It was about being half-Polish and half-English, and the things I'd told him about speaking Polish until I was six and then forgetting it all:

> *"Mother, I've lost the words you gave me.*
> *Call the police, tell them*
> *there's a reward, I'll do anything. . ."*

He was going to put it in the literary magazine, *"if you hare no objection, Carla"*. That was the way he wrote, always very polite. I said it was fine by me.

One day the Head stopped me and said, "Did you ever write to that chap? The Polish teacher?"

"Yes," I said. Nothing more. Let him think I'd written once then not bothered. Luckily, Mrs Callendar came up to talk about OFSTED.

"Ah, yes, OFSTED. Speaking of visitors," said the Head, raising his voice the way he does so that one minute he's talking to you and the next it's a public announcement, "I have news of progress on the Polish teachers' exchange. A teacher will be coming over from Katowice next month. His name is Stefan Jeziorny, and he will be staying with Mrs Kenward. We're most grateful to you for your hospitality, Valerie."

Mrs Kenward flushed. The Head beamed at nobody. Stefan Jeziorny, I thought. I had clicked, even though I was so used to thinking of him as Steve. Why hadn't he said he was coming?

I dropped Jade off to tea with her friend. There was a letter waiting when I got home. I tore it open and read it with my coat still on. There was a bit about my last letter, and poetry, and then the news.

"You will know from your school, Carla, that I will come to England. I am hoping to make many contacts for the future, for other teachers who will also come to English schools. I hope, Carla, that you will introduce me to your colleagues. I will stay with an English Family who offer accommodation."

I felt terrible. He sounded different, not like Steve. Not just polite any more, but all stiff, and a bit hurt. He must have thought I'd known about his visit from the other teachers, and I hadn't wanted to invite him to stay with me. But what was worse was that he was going to expect to meet me. Or not me, exactly, but the person he'd been writing to, who didn't really exist. *"I have been corresponding with a colleague of yours, Carla Carter,"* he'd say to the other teachers. Then he'd wait for someone to say, *"Yes, of course, Carla's here, she's expecting you."*

Colleagues don't wear blue overalls and white caps and work for £3.89 an hour. Somebody'd remember me asking the Head for his address, and there'd be a whisper running all round, followed by a horrible silence. They'd all look round at the serving-hatch and there I'd be, the big teapot in my hand and a plate of buns in front of me. And Steve'd look too. He'd still be smiling, because that's what you do in a foreign place when you don't know what's going on.

He'd think I was trying to make a fool of him, making him believe I was a teacher. Me, Carla Carter, part-time catering assistant, writing to him about poetry.

I could be off sick. I could swap with Jeannie. She could do the teachers' breaks. Or I could say Jade was ill.

No. That wouldn't work. Steve had my name, and my address. I sat down and spread out his letter again, then I went to the drawer and got all his other letters. I'd never had letters like that before and I was never going to again, not after Steve knew who I really was.

I didn't write, and Steve didn't write again either. I couldn't decide if it was because he was hurt, or because he knew he'd be seeing me soon anyway. The fuss Valerie Kenward made about having him to stay, you'd think the Pope was coming for a fortnight. I never liked her. Always holding up the queue saying she's on a diet, and then taking the biggest bun.

"If you're that bothered," I said, "he can come and stay in my flat, with me and Jade." But I said it to myself, in my head. I knew he'd want to be with the other teachers.

I couldn't stop looking for letters. And then there was the poetry book I'd bought. It seemed a shame to bin it. It might come in for Jade, I thought.

A week went by, eight days, ten. Each morning I woke up and I knew something was wrong before I could remember what it was. It got worse every day until I thought, *Sod it, I'm not going to worry any more.*

The next morning-break the buns were stale. Valerie Kenward poked them, one after another. "We ought to get our money back," she said. But she still took one, and waited while I filled the teapot from the urn.

"How's it going?" Susie Douglas asked her.

"*Hard work!*" stage-whispered Valerie, rolling her eyes.

"He's not got much conversation, then?"

"Are you joking? All he wants to talk about is poetry. It's hell for the kids, he doesn't mean to be funny but they can't keep a straight face. It's the way he talks. Philippa had to leave the room at supper-time, and I can't say I blame her."

You wouldn't, I thought. If ever anyone brought up their kids to be pleased with themselves, it's Valerie Kenward.

"And even when it's quite a well-known writer like Shakespeare or Shelley, you can't make out what he's on about. It's the accent."

"He *is* Polish. I mean, how many Polish poets could you pronounce?" asked Susie.

"And his *ties*!" went on Valerie. "You've never seen anything like them."

I looked past both of them. I'd have noticed him before, if I hadn't been so busy. He was sitting stiffly upright, smiling in the way people smile when they don't quite understand what's going on. The Head was wagging a sheaf of papers in front of him, and talking very loudly, as if he was deaf. Steve. Stefan Jeziorny. He was wearing a brown suit with padded shoulders. It looked too big for him. His tie was wider than normal ties, and it was red with bold green squiggles on it. It was a terribly hopeful tie. His shoes had a fantastic shine on them. His face looked much too open, much too alive, as if a child Jade's age had got into an adult's body.

"Isn't that tea made *yet*?" asked Valerie.

I looked at her. "No," I said. "It's not. Excuse me," and I lifted the counter-flap and ducked past her while her mouth was still open. I walked up to where Steve was sitting. He looked round at me the way a child does when he doesn't know anyone at a party, hoping for rescue.

"Hello," I said. He jumped up, held out his hand. "How do you do?" he asked, as if he really wanted to know. I took his hand. It was sweaty, as I'd known it would be. He was tense as a guitar string.

"I'm Carla," I said.

"Carla?" He couldn't hide anything. I saw it all swim in his eyes. Surprise. Uncertainty. What was he going to do? And then I saw it. Pleasure. A smile lit in his eyes and ran to his mouth.

"Carla! You are Carla Carter. My penfriend."

"Yes."

Then he did something I still can't quite believe. He stood there holding on to my hand right in the middle of the staff-room, his big bright tie blazing, and he sang a song I knew. It went through me like a knife through butter. A Polish song. I knew it, I knew it. I knew the words and the tune. It was one of the songs my mother used to sing to me. I felt my lips move. There were words in my mouth, words I didn't understand. And then I was singing, stumbling after him all the way to the end of the verse.

"Good heavens. How very remarkable. I didn't realize you were Polish, Mrs . . . er . . ." said the Head as he bumbled round us flapping his papers.

"Nor did I," I said. But I wasn't going to waste time on the Head. I wanted to talk about poetry. I smiled at Steve. His red tie with its bold green squiggles was much too wide and much too bright. It was a flag from another country, a better country than the ones either of us lived in. "I like your tie," I said.

Lilac

There were two springs that year. The first was in London, where we lived, and where my mother was breaking down into a thousand pieces. But I didn't know that. I was thirteen, and although I guessed a lot, I wasn't capable of believing this could really be happening to the person who'd taught me everything about optimism since I was born. My father seemed to want to tell me something all the time, but I wouldn't let him. And then one night he said I was going to stay with my Aunt Birgit for three months. It was only May.

"But I'll miss school," I said.

He rubbed his nose hard. "You can manage without school," he said. "You'll have Agnes and Tommy."

These were my cousins. I used to know them quite well, but I hadn't seen them since I was eleven, and as you know, everything happens between the ages of eleven and thirteen.

"You'll learn to speak Swedish," he said, and then he said something more in Swedish which I didn't understand. He'd always spoken English with us, perfect English, by far the most perfect in the house.

The lilacs came out for the second time in Aunt Birgit's garden. Aunt Birgit and Uncle Mikael lived in a small town about three hours north of Stockholm, in a wooden house with a big wild garden. I loved the birchwood fence that enclosed it. It made me feel that for all the wildness, and the hundreds of miles of forest marching north and east, I was safe. The lilacs were tight-packed cones of flower-bud.

My cousin Agnes was six now, and even I could see how beautiful she was. She had big green eyes and silvery, feathery hair, but she hardly ever spoke. There was a playhouse in the garden, and she spent most of her time in there with her dolls and friends and secrets, whispering and laughing. She knew a few words of English, and I knew a bit of Swedish, but not enough to talk to her. Tommy was fifteen, two years older than me.

I loved Tommy. Of course I did, it was natural. We were the same kind of person. We liked fishing and biking and climbing trees and arguing about books we'd read and swimming naked in the river late in the evening when it was still light. Swedish people are different about their bodies. They don't care about being naked the way English people do. I didn't care either. We were both thin and dark and strong. Tommy never asked any questions about my mother: he seemed to take it for granted that I was here for the summer.

There were lots of empty times. Tommy and Agnes were at school in the day, my Aunt Birgit was a radiographer at the hospital, and my Uncle Mikael was working on a social-research project based in Stockholm. Aunt Birgit kept trying to arrange things for me, but I was fine at home. I lay on my bed reading and listening to music, or I wandered round the garden. Once

I clambered into Agnes's playhouse. It was dry and cool and it smelled of sweet new wood, and I curled up as if I was lying inside a walnut shell. Through the little window I saw the new leaves flash and rustle. Everything was coming alive, and it was the fastest, greenest spring I had ever seen.

The next day, at breakfast, Tommy said to me, "I've got a friend coming for the weekend. His name is Henrik."

Agnes flashed a look at me and said something. Aunt Birgit translated. "She says that Henrik is the best hockey player in Tommy's school." Aunt Birgit smiled again, just for me. "Agnes thinks Henrik is wonderful."

"She means ice-hockey, Christie," said Tommy. He sounded offhand but I knew he didn't mean it. Henrik coming was important. And then something made me look across the table, and there was Uncle Mikael, quite still, looking at Tommy. It was his stillness that had made me turn. But Tommy didn't notice.

I went out on to the porch, into the sun. The birds were singing so sharply it hurt. I ran down the steps, through the long wet grass and birch trees, to the grove of bird-cherries that was out of sight of the house. The bird-cherries would blossom soon, Uncle Mikael said. They froth up and then they're gone. I wanted to see it. I wanted to see everything. I threw myself down on to the ground and sniffed the smell of my own warm skin, and the wild garlic I'd crushed in lying down. Then I rolled on my back and stared up through the branches of the bird-cherries.

"The lilac is my favourite flower," Aunt Birgit had said yesterday, pulling down a branch to touch the tight buds that were flushed with colour now, but not yet ready to open, not yet scented. "Do you have lilacs at home, Christie?"

"No," I said.

She misunderstood me, thinking I meant there were no lilacs in England. "Ah, I couldn't live without them," she said. "Lilacs, to me, are spring."

I told myself I'd keep out of the way when Henrik came. They'd want to talk about school, and ice- hockey, and other things I didn't know about. And they'd probably want to talk in Swedish, too. I walked slowly back up to the house. Aunt Birgit met me, dressed in her work clothes.

"Listen to those chaffinches," she said. "Did you ever hear birds make so much noise?" I listened. It was wild and harsh, not like singing at all.

"I didn't know they were chaffinches," I said.

"I think it is the right word," said Aunt Birgit. She was very proud of her English.

"No, I meant —" But I didn't go on. I wanted to hug her, tight, tight, and I wanted to run away from her, all at the same time. My father and Aunt Birgit are twins, but they don't look alike.

Aunt Birgit put her hand on my hair. "You must tell me, Christie," she said, "if there is anything you want."

And then it was the weekend. Henrik was coming at six o'clock. I'd offered to go in with Agnes, but it was all right, Aunt Birgit said. Henrik would sleep in Tommy's room. Tommy was lying on the porch swing, his eyes nearly closed, his legs sprawled out over the faded canvas cushions. He looked as if he was falling asleep. But when I sat down beside him I knew he wasn't. He was tense as a fishing-line when there's the first thrum of a bite.

It was warm, really warm for the first time. The sound of the birds was softer today, more liquid. We watched a big wood-pigeon in the apple-tree, standing on a branch and pulling at the flower-buds. From time to time it stared at us and purred, deep in its throat. Suddenly Tommy sat forward. He'd heard something I hadn't. A moment later I heard the gate swing back against the post.

"It's him," breathed out Tommy, as if he was talking to himself.

"Henrik?"

"Yes."

We were both silent, listening for footsteps. But Henrik must have stepped off the gravel on to the mossy grass, because suddenly there he was, dappled with sun and shielding his eyes with one hand as he looked up at the porch. He carried a sports bag.

"Henrik, hi, come on up," said Tommy in the rather American way he spoke English. The words sounded relaxed, but the voice wasn't. "This is my cousin, my English cousin Christie. She doesn't speak Swedish."

Henrik smiled at me as he swung up the steps to the porch. He dropped the bag on to the bleached wooden planking, and then, completely without self-consciousness, he stretched and yawned as if he had just woken up.

That was Henrik. He was one of those people who is easy in life, as if it's his own element. I noticed it, because I wasn't like that, except when I was running or swimming or sitting for long quiet hours by the water. He said the right things to everyone, but it wasn't planned. He helped Aunt Birgit to work out how to make a conference call on her new telephone system. He pored over Uncle Mikael's plans for a pond in the garden. Agnes showed him secret things she wouldn't show to anyone else. And I waited, and I knew that Tommy was waiting too.

The first night I lay awake. I could hear Henrik and Tommy talking in Tommy's room on the other side of the wall, talking and talking. Sometimes their voices would stop and I'd relax and begin to drift away, then I'd hear them again. It wasn't that I wanted to know what they were saying. It was all in Swedish anyway. But I couldn't sleep. The house seemed to float in the nearly-dark of the May evening, and the blue-and-white curtains Aunt Birgit had made for me stirred in the warm breeze, as if something outside was breathing.

We were at the lake all the next day. I thought Henrik and Tommy would want to go off on their own, but Henrik said at breakfast, "We're all going on a fishing trip today, Mrs Larsson. We'll look after Christie." And he smiled at me as if to say, *We have to talk like that for the sake of the adults. I know that you can look after yourself. You are one of us.*

I don't remember much about the day. Only the sun, the still, black waters of the lake we went to, the sandwiches of smoked reindeer tongue which I couldn't bring myself to eat. We came back dazed with air, and the glitter of sun on water. It was too bright and the fishing was no good, but I didn't care. I cycled behind Henrik, watching him.

The second night the lilacs were fully open. It was even warmer, and this time there were no voices coming through the wall. They must have been so tired that they fell asleep straight away. But I couldn't sleep. I got up and kneeled on the window-seat. There was a three-quarter moon rising, and then a bird called, as if it thought it was morning. I had to be outside.

My bare feet brushed the wooden floors so that I felt like a ghost. The porch looked strange in moonlight, with shadows that folded away differently. I went down the cold wooden steps, on to the grass, and then I smelled lilac on the air. It came faintly, and then strong. I wanted to be close to it and to pull down the branches as Aunt Birgit had done. I wanted to bury my face in the flowers. I walked silently through wet grass that tickled my ankles, towards the lilac bushes.

There they were. Henrik and Tommy, so close they looked not like two people but like a new creature which no one had seen before. But I recognized them. I didn't cry out, I didn't make a sound. They were under the lilacs, as if they'd grown there. They didn't see me, or anything else. I saw Tommy, his head back, his eyes closed, and Henrik kissing his throat.

The next day, when the sun was high, I went back to the lilac bushes. There was no sign except a patch of trampled grass. I pulled down a branch and buried my face in the cones of flower. The smell of the lilacs went through me as if my blood was carrying it. Strong, sweet, languid, yet fresh as water. I shut my eyes. I thought of Uncle Mikael and the way he had watched Tommy, quite still. I thought of Aunt Birgit. *"Lilacs, to me, are spring. I couldn't live without them."*

I said nothing.

You Stayed Awake with Me

Six a.m.

"Here you are. Tea."

Janet opens the curtains and looks at the day. We don't care how early it is, as long as it's morning. The grey light curls in like smoke. I know how it will be out there. Montbretia and foxgloves wet in the hedges, the cows going down the lane like boats, barging into one another. Shit-streaks on their legs, tails switching.

Janet knows how much I want the night to be over. Even late-night radio doesn't work after a while. You're stuck on Planet Night, with the sound turned down low and voice talking to naked voice in the darkness. You want the light on, but then it's not worth moving because any moment now you'll be asleep again.

My dreams wait for me. It's like a game of statues. When I look, they won't move. When I turn my back, they swarm all over me. I dream, and when I come back I don't remember anything. And the radio's still playing the same tune.

Terry Matthias is my favourite. He croons me through the night with his stories about a bus he caught that went miles off its route with all the passengers too polite to say so, or about a dish his grandma used to make when he was a little boy. And I want to write to him, humble and grateful, the sort of silly letter women must send him from every corner of the country. All I'll say is, *You stayed awake with me.*

The pain was bad last night. I could have stood up and peeled out my spine from my flesh like the spine of a salmon. Lift it up, take it away from where it hurts. Though it's not really my spine that's the problem, I know that. My body's turned on itself. First of all my finger-joints, shiny and red and swollen so that none of my rings fit. Then my elbows, my ankles, my knees. I've had cortisone injections, and gold. Nothing turns off the switch that's been thrown wrong. *It's your body's auto-immune system*, they say, as if this has nothing to do with me. I want to ask them who they think they are talking to, if not to my body? But I would swallow anything for the sake of waking up and not knowing, for a second of bliss, that I had a body at all. Next week I'm going into hospital for further tests.

"I put sugar in it," says Janet. "Here, I've got your tablets."

Together we hoist me up and Janet buffs the pillows so I can lean back, drink the tea, swallow the tablets.

"The dust," she says. "Wait a minute."

I wait, gazing out of the window which has no curtains. There's a heavenly square of sky, grey slipping into blue. It'll be hot later, though the garden will be knee-deep wet now. Dew on the big dockleaves, dew slapping your legs as you go down to the privy. This garden is full of goosegrass, bindweed, dock. Only the roses on the wall are tough enough to keep on flowering. And the rosemary, of course, and a rough branch of sage. All that's left of my mother's garden.

But I don't have to think about that. I can lie back on the white pillow Janet brought down in her car along with all the other stuff.

We've escaped. We're two women in a semi-derelict cottage with no telephone. Or are we? I don't think we've come to a full-stop at all. I think we're still travelling.

Janet comes in with a broom and a dish of water. She dips her hand into the water and scatters drops of it all over the floorboards like a priest asperging the congregation. A drop hits my lips. I taste it, and wonder if the water still tastes different down here, as we always said it did. Our hands under the outside tap. Water bulging in our cupped palms, and running over. The gollopy noise of Janet drinking.

Janet begins to sweep the dampening dust. It smells like the first drops of rain, when a storm comes at the end of a baking August afternoon.

"There," says Janet, "that's better."

I nod. It is.

"Sit on the bed," I say. I want Janet to stay with me, as I always wanted my mother to stay with me when I was ill as a child. *I'll just take the rubbish out first*, she'd say. *I'll make your bed nice. I'll fetch you a drink.*

But Janet simply stays. I take her hand between my ugly swollen fingers, and hold it. Janet's hand is warm, and moist from the effort of sweeping out the room. Her skin isn't smooth, it's rough at the finger-ends, from the chemicals she uses in her darkroom.

"Janet," I say. I need to go to the toilet. I think of the stairs. It's worst in the morning, but the more you move, even if it's painful, the better it gets. I am supposed to keep moving. But I'm afraid of the grit that's settled in my joints overnight, ready to grind into my raw flesh as soon as I move.

We're halfway down the stairs. Janet is ahead of me, watching in case I fall. I can't straighten myself and I'm nauseous with the pain. It passes.

"Is it bad?" Janet asks.

"Better," I say, because I know it will be, if I can just keep moving down the four remaining stairs, over the strip of rush matting and through the kitchen to the back door.

But halfway down the garden path I know I'm not going to do it. Sweat starts out all over me.

"Get a chair," I tell her. Janet runs into the cottage and comes back with one of the kitchen chairs. I sit down and slowly everything settles. I try to picture all the cells of my body settling, not fighting one another till they are red and roaring with pain. I sit as still as I can, with my feet in the wet grass and the legs of the chair unsteady on the path. Janet squats in front of me with a cup of water and slants it to my lips so I can swallow.

"We should have left it longer, to give your tablets time to work," she says.

I shake my head slightly. It doesn't matter. Now that I'm safely on the chair, it seems as good a place as any to spend the day. Soon the sun will begin to dry the dew off the leaves, and the snails will creep back into the shelter of broken flower-pots by the wall. And that

21

thrush, looking at me so boldly, wondering if it dare come close enough to seize the snail I'm looking at and hammer out its life against a stone — it'll fly off.

"Janet," I say, "what if I can't ever have a baby? All that stuff they're giving me. I'm packed full of chemicals."

"Did they say anything?"

"No. I didn't ask."

"You'll be better," says Janet. "You'll be able to think about it then. Don't think about it now."

I like being told not to think about things. Janet has two children, a boy called Lucas and a girl called Mary. Already they are twelve and fourteen, old enough for Janet to leave with their father for a week.

"Why is it, do you think, that you've ended up with children and I haven't?" I ask.

But Janet doesn't answer. She knows I'm not complaining. Or even wanting an answer, although I ask.

Noon

I'm under the tamarisks, in the shade, shelling peas. This is just the kind of activity which is good for my hands. *Use it or lose it*, they keep telling me at physio sessions. But the pea-pods have a mind of their own and they explode peas into the long grass where I can't reach them. Janet is inside, making sandwiches. There she is, moving as surely as if she's in her own kitchen. She passes and repasses the kitchen window, looking as if she's always been here, and has never gone away at all.

All the picnics we've made in that kitchen. First my mother making sandwiches for everyone. Ham sandwiches in greaseproof paper, and hard-boiled eggs with a black line around the yolks. We were little then, and we got in her way, pouring salt over the table while Mum made her paper screws of salt to take with us. Mum sent us out to sit on the doorstep and wait for her. Always the stone of the doorstep was cold. We played for hours, it seemed, rolling up woodlice and racing snails. High above us Mum said, "Mind still, girls," and her skirt tickled our faces as she stepped over us.

Every summer from the time we were three, Janet came down and spent a month with us. There's a photo of us, sitting on the doorstep, arms round each other's shoulders, offering our closeness to the camera, our smiles squinting our eyes shut. Janet and me, me and Janet. Janet's mother was Mum's oldest friend, and we were following where they'd already been. But Janet's mother couldn't stay, because she'd married a man who didn't want her to have friends. All she had were the days of bringing Janet, and the days of taking her away again. She and my mother sat in the sun, their bare legs spread.

When Janet was with us, we all seemed better than we were. She took in our lives and gave them back to us, brighter and bolder than before. In her shadow I grew wild. It was a wildness I loved, because it made my father laugh. It was Janet who taught me French skipping, and proper breaststroke, and how to pick up jellyfish on a spade and carry them deep into the sea so they would swim away. We never actually saw them

23

swim away, but they would float there willingly, their purple tentacles dangling like baby legs. It's possible that there were things I taught Janet, too, but I don't remember them. Once we saw a dead porpoise, with words carved into his flesh.

I loved my father. I was wild for him. He could never come for the whole summer, but for ten days, or two weeks, he belonged entirely to us. Or so I thought each year, before he came. My mother would expect him too, building him up for us. She didn't drive, but when he came we'd be able to go all over. It wasn't worth buying steak for three, but when Dad came we'd have steak, fried onions, and fried potatoes. We'd drink beer out of his glass, and then we'd stay up late, past the end of the long western summer dusks. We'd walk on our hands in the garden, while my parents drank and murmured. Sometimes we'd get dizzy from the beer, and collapse on our backs on the damp grass where the dew was beginning to fall. We'd look up where the sky was darkening, and the first stars were coming out, first one then more and more, thickening over the sky. We'd feel the earth spin under us, and the stars draw us up.

The first morning Dad was here we'd get up early and stream off over the three fields and two stiles we had to cross before we came to the steep, scrambling path down to the sea. We'd see the myxie rabbits and my father would say, "Don't look at them. There's nothing you can do for them."

Down at the sea there was no one. The tide far out, the beach glistening with cold, fresh sand. Tracks of birds, suck of crabs digging down backwards into their holes as we came. The wet, bubbling stream that broke out icily from the rocks at the side of the bay. A place by those rocks to nest in with our towels.

And then the swimming. We scarcely saw our hideous swimsuits as we dragged them on, gritty with yesterday's sand. Janet was my horse as we raced down the beach. And the thing was not to stop, not even to change pace as we plunged on into the water, kicking our way through the thigh-deep waves. And then we'd stumble and go down with a wave on top of us, so sudden that sometimes I didn't even have time to shut my eyes. My father would not watch us while we swam. He would close his eyes, leaning back against his rock, and only open them when we pelted back to him, showering off sparks of salt water on to his flesh. I'd jump about and boast about how far I'd swum. One day, I thought, I'd swim so far that he'd miss me and sit up, shading his face to see where I was. And there I'd be, far out, a tiny dot making for the headland. And there he'd be —

Maybe he would rescue me. Or maybe he would lie back again, and shut his eyes against the light. But I could hear for sure my mother's angry, frightened voice. *"Don't encourage her. She's only doing it to show off."* And I could see the way she'd pace up and down at the edge of the water, knee-deep, her face rucked with fear.

My mother couldn't swim.

Each night we licked our knees in the bath for the taste of salt. I was skinnier and darker than Janet, and my hair was cut so that a skim of shampoo and a duck under the water would get the sea out of it. But Janet took her time, frowning as she undid her plaits and combed out the tangles. When her hair stood out around her head like a bush she squeezed out just the right amount of toothpaste, and cleaned her teeth as white as pearls. It half maddened me to watch her cleaning the inside of her teeth, and then the back, then spitting, then rinsing, then spitting again, as if there could be no other way of doing things. But at the same time I liked to watch her.

Janet comes out, holding a wide wooden tray. There are prawn sandwiches, and smoked-mackerel sandwiches with lemon juice. There is ginger cake, a bowl of grapes, and a wedge of Cheddar. Janet went to the shops this morning to buy everything. I listened to her car going away down the lane, and I sat in the following silence, and was afraid.

"You're not eating," Janet says.

"It's all the stuff in my body. It screws up your appetite." I eat the grapes, one by one. Their skins are stretched tight as the skins of little porkers, then they burst and spray the juice inside my mouth. But the grapes are slippery and I keep dropping them.

"Your father," says Janet.

"What?"

"I was just thinking," says Janet. Then, "Do you want a drink?"

"Yes," I say immediately. I want not just to drink, but to get drunk. Never mind if I can't, because the drugs don't let me. Janet goes inside, and when she returns she's got an old green bottle with a handwritten label on it. I recognize it, and I also see that Janet's wiped it carefully of dust.

"Blackberry wine," says Janet.

"My mother made it."

"I know."

All those bottles, stored up to be given away.

"It's nice. Strong."

"Yeah."

It is thick and dark, not fruity any more. I drink a glass and it seems to lift off the top layer of my skin. I pour another. Janet lies back, crushing the grass, and slits her eyes against the June brightness. I swallow more of the wine.

"Do you love me?" I ask. My voice comes out harsh, almost barking.

"You know I do."

"Do you want to know how Dad is?"

Janet rolls over, props herself on her elbows, looks at me. "You know I do," she says again.

"He's in an apartment in Florida. He plays golf. He always eats that special spread that reduces his cholesterol level, because Betty Marie won't have anything else in the house."

"How do you know? About the cholesterol spread, I mean."

"He tells me."

"Imagine you talking about that," says Janet. "Out of all those things you used to talk about."

"Where did it happen?" I ask suddenly, quick as a knife in the dark.

"What?"

"You know. Him and you."

"You already know," says Janet. "You know it was here."

"Here," I say. "Yes, but where here? By that wall? In their bedroom? In the toilet, standing up? Or here, exactly here? Just where we're sitting now?"

"No," says Janet. "Not exactly here."

"But you remember."

"Of course."

It's the next day I remember. My parents' voices low and stern in the bedroom, as if they were discussing an operation. The sheer blue of the sky blazing, unattended. Janet saying, "Let's go for a walk." As we walked she frowned as if the sun was too bright for her. She picked heads of clover and dropped them without sucking the flowers for honey, as we always did. We never picked flowers just to throw them away. We climbed the Beacon and then Janet said, "I'm going home."

There were three weeks and four days of our holiday still to run. I thought she was joking. No, I didn't think she was joking. I thought the world had slipped sideways, like a crazy picture.

"I'm going back to pack my case," said Janet.

So when my mother and father came out together, the married couple, Janet was already fitting together the inner clasp on her case. Her things were packed as neatly as ever, her shoes toe to heel in plastic bags. She'd changed for the journey, and walked up to the pub to order the taxi. And now she said to my parents, "I'm afraid I have to go back home unexpectedly."

And they said nothing for a while. Then my mother took a step forward with her hands outstretched, and said, "Are you sure, Janet? Are you sure you can't stay?" She sounded plaintive, just as she sounded when she made a chicken pie and there was half of it left over.

"No," Janet said. "I have to go now."

Now I see them. My father not as he is now, but as he was then. He has got hold of Janet and he is grasping her with an adult, fierce closeness. And although she's got her head flung back, it's not to push him off but to let his lips fasten on her white throat. Her hands hang at her sides, not yet grasping him back, but open-palmed, yielding. I know that they are warm, and moist. My father, not self-possessed any more, but sweating, fierce, his face screwed into a mask I don't recognize. And as Janet's left hand flicks up blindly, she says, "Yes," under her breath. But not too quietly for me to hear it.

We are fifteen. We are young for our ages, or I think we have been. Then Janet's mouth opens, and shows the white teeth she has kept so clean for years, and she says, "Yes," meaning it.

"I thought I'd never be able to come back here," says Janet.

Next year, no Janet, and I was sixteen. The following year we let the cottage to strangers. It was my mother's, and she had the right to do with it as she wanted. She let it go year by year, the roof not slated, the wiring not checked, the damp spreading across the wall which hugged the hill. My mother had been born in that room, but it seemed to mean nothing to her any more. Her one concession was not to sell it.

"Did you tell your mother?" I ask Janet now.

"Of course not."

The pain is getting strong again. Pain is a climate like winter. It closes over you and soon you can't imagine not living in it. Some days, when I wake, before I move, I pretend to myself. I think I've got away. I'm stepping off a plane into a different climate where warm, spicy breezes blow your clothes against your thighs. I'm walking so lightly and easily that it feels like flying.

Ten p.m.

It's nearly dark. A greenish June dusk, hay-scented and succulent.

"I want to see the sea," I say.

"We could drive down."

"I want to walk," I say.

I know I won't be able to walk over the three fierds and two stiles, but perhaps I can get as far as the end of the first field. There's a stone stile, and through the gap you can see the sea.

We'll go in the morning, early, before anyone else is up. The only people we'll risk meeting are ourselves.

There they go. They race past without a glance. All they are thinking about is the next stile, the next field, the damp, sandy swimsuits that slap from their hands, the sudden scent of convolvulus crushed underfoot, the big jellyfish that came into the bay last night, the chocolate in Janet's pocket and the water that will close over them and kill their ears with its rapid drumming. They stare, their faces blank and bright, not registering us.

"We'll go tomorrow," I say. I'm too tired to explain what I really mean. I lie back and the stars fall away from me, as they used to fall.

"Yes," says Janet.

"Do you really think we can get there?"

"Yes," says Janet, as I know she always will.

The Fag

You've been driving a long time without a break, in thick traffic. But you pass a slip road where most of the traffic peels off and is not replaced, and suddenly the motorway opens out ahead of you. You are driving westward. It's been raining all day, but before it gets dark a few seconds of sunset will squeeze out from under those clouds. The Levels are hectic green. There is so much water in them that the rhynes can't carry it away. Sedge, willow, rhyne. In their flatness a few square-towered churches hang, suspended. Near to Exeter the motorway turns pink, and here are the small, clumpy, thick-hedged Devon fields, like dolls' fields. Too luscious: it makes you want to sleep. But you're going to keep on going, through barer and barer ground, over Dartmoor, past Indian Kings and Indian Queens, past wind farms and china clay spoil-heaps and blue plastic fertilizer bags blowing on barbed wire.

You've got to have a fag. Can you get one without asking for it? You keep looking straight ahead where another slick of rain dashes down over the motorway. You take your left hand off the wheel and hold it up, the first two fingers slightly apart. Of course he guesses at once. This is what he does. Quickly takes the fag out of its fresh, moist pack. Doesn't bother with the car-lighter because you hate the electric taste of it. Strikes a match, lets the flame wobble and settle, puts the fag in his own mouth, lights it with the tiniest drag so as not to spoil the freshness of it for you (you know all this without looking), puts the fag between your fingers. You take the first drag. The smell of it was always going to be more wonderful than the taste, but you knew that. You take in the smoke and you're dizzy, looking through the slosh of wipers on rain to the road which is quiet now, but still needs to be watched.

You feel light. You're not driving any more, you're floating. The sky ahead holds the kind of brightness which lets you know the sea is close. Lots of sea, more of it than you'll ever need, stretching all the way to America. The sea is your wilderness. Living on this tight little island where everything you see has been built or planted, you look west to discover what you want and haven't got. It is what you dream of. Crowded with mackerel and porpoises, seaweed and catfish, streams of salmon with their destinations wired into their brains, minke whale, and the twenty-foot basking shark you once thought would upset your boat. But empty, too. The sea throws off everything. You walk on its crackling scurf of polystyrene and plastic tampon applicators. You think of whales, and the buffalo that made the plains boom under their million hooves. You think of Vachel Lindsay writing about the flower-fed buffaloes.

But they are gone. You think of a dolphin losing its way and swimming into the Thames, under Westminster Bridge. You realize how much longer all these things will live than you will: the bridge, the river, the packed addresses north and south of it. Even the whales turning in the deep. Even the polystyrene.

But you are still in the car, driving. You take a second drag, a deeper one. The fag has lost its virginal sweetness. The tobacco is toasted now, its taste muddied by the filter. You remember untipped Navy Cut, a carton of it, duty-free. You remember rolling your own Golden Virginia out of a two-ounce tin, and the smell of the tobacco when you tore off the green-and-white band and unwrapped the gold paper. Then all the way back to Peter Stuyvesant and early Consulates, cool as a mountain stream. The river of money you've smoked in your life.

The texture of the road changes from Tarmac to concrete. He hands you the cigarettes. You take them, smoke them.

You've gone past your turn-off. You don't, in fact, know where you are going, or how to get back. You take your left hand off the wheel.

Leonardo, Michelangelo, SuperStork

No one should be eight-and-a-half months pregnant in the middle of the hottest summer for ten years. Already the papers are disputing records, and blazing extra breasts amid thinned-out news coverage.

In their neighbouring houses, Susie and Pat walk from airless room to airless room. Their flesh chafes against their maternity support bras. They count days, but each hour swells, like their breasts and bellies, until it seems as if time has stopped. There is only the relentless present. Their parched, tawny gardens are unbearable, except at night, when moths cling to windows and music thuds from distant parties. Somewhere, there are slender, unencumbered people still drinking and dancing.

"Not long to go," people say encouragingly, or, with sharper truth, "You might as well make the most of it. After all, you'll be paying for it for the rest of your life." Pat grimaces in response. She cannot find a smile at the thought of the mountainous second mortgage she and Clinton have had to take on in order to pay for this child. She's worked out, grimly, that each day of her pregnancy is costing them three hundred pounds. A trickle of sweat finds the most inaccessible channel down her back. She frowns, multiplying and dividing in her head, then frowns again as she sees Susie next door standing in the middle of her patch of grass, her arms hanging down idle, her face turned up to the annihilating whiteness of the sun.

With skin like that, Susie should take care. Pat congratulates herself, knowing that her own baby has no genetic tendency towards skin cancer. To comfort herself after calculating her debt, she goes, as she always does, to the drawer where she and Clinton keep the brochure. And there he is, her baby, smiling up at her from a sheepskin rug. One hand grasps a rattle, and waves it, as if in greeting. His smile is wide, showing his two upper and two lower teeth. The photograph cannot show his intelligence quotient, his sparkling genes, his eventual height and weight, his shoe size, his right-handedness, his excellent hand-eye coordination, or his absence of sociopathic tendencies. It does not need to: all these are carefully listed, and guaranteed, along with a mass of detail which is almost too much for Pat and Clinton to take in.

Their boy. With him comes an assurance that cloning has been strictly limited. In addition, a unique feature of the Michelangelo service is that the peer group has been geographically dispersed, using computer modelling to assess parental relocation probabilities. Their little one can bask in his individuality, with no risk of meeting his own likeness at the local toddler group.

You have to pay, if you want the best, Pat reassures herself. There are cheaper services, but the Michelangelo is a cut above. Her friend Carol used

SuperStork, but then she only got a local when they removed her Rubicon. Pat shivers in spite of the heat, crossing her legs at the memory of raw pain when she woke from her own general anaesthetic. After the baby was born they would have to fit her Rubicon again, and this time it would stay there, for they would never be able to afford another seventy thousand pounds. You did see people who had two children; three, even; but not around here.

Susie lugs the hose over the dry garden. *It's all right, I have a licence for it*, she wants to call across to Pat's silent, disapproving windows. She must make sure to mention the fact some time. "My water bill! If this goes on we'll have to give up the hosepipe licence."

Susie is afraid of Pat. She looks into the mirror of Pat's pregnancy, and fears that it will give back a true image of her own, an image which Pat will be able to read. She watches the hose grow taut, and water spill on to her flower-bed. Dust kicks up from the dry soil, then the water darkens it. The garden smells acrid, stormy. Susie goes back over that last conversation with Pat, over and over.

"Wasn't it the worst part, having your Rubicon removed?" Pat had asked.

"The worst pain I've had in my life," answered Susie, without thinking.

"Oh God — did you only have a local then, like Carol? I couldn't face that. It was one of the reasons we went for the Michelangelo. Are you with SuperStork as well, then?"

"No, no, I'm —"And Susie's mind froze. She simply could not remember the word. It was there, locked in her brain, but she couldn't reach it. "No, I'm with —" She had it. "Leonardo."

She had named the most expensive, the classiest of the services. They had decided on that deliberately, to make it unlikely that any of their neighbours would be fellow-clients. The Leonardo service cost over a hundred thousand pounds, but for that you bought an embryo whose name might be seen in lights. If the environmental factors were right, of course, but that was down to you.

"The Leonardo?" Pat's face had contracted. "Really? And they didn't give you a general?"

"Afterwards, I mean," explained Susie hastily. "The pain was afterwards." She put out of her mind the little whitewashed room where she had opened her legs to a sympathetic medical student. It was the first Rubicon he'd ever removed, and he was clumsy. He sweated and she saw him sweat, in fear for herself as well as in fear of the law. Besides the mandatory prison sentence and confiscation of personal property, no violator of the Genetic Code could ever be considered for embryo implantation.

She had watched jealousy and curiosity fight on Pat's face, but no more had been said. Later, she'd talked to Reuben far into the night, fearfully drawing out and examining every strand of the conversation.

Water runs into her sandals, and Susie jerks back to the present. She looks up, and there is Pat, watching across the knee-high gesture of a fence.

"You were miles away. Thinking about the baby?"

"Mmm. I must just go and turn the hose off."

She goes around the side of the house and turns off the tap, but when she comes back Pat is still there.

"Me, too," says Pat. "I keep looking at the brochure. Silly, isn't it?"

"Yes."

"He's so beautiful. I can't believe he's really mine."

"I know."

Pat puts her hands over the cotton mound of her belly, and the knob of her protruding navel. "We shouldn't grumble about the heat. After all, this'll never come again, will it?"

"No."

There's a little breeze, or maybe it is only the freshness of watered earth. The sun is beginning to slip down the sky at last, ripening from white to yellow, turning Pat's neat little face golden. The women stand for a moment, saying nothing. Both feel their babies kick. Then Pat turns towards Susie. Nakedly, her face offers a confidence.

"Do you want to see him? Shall I bring out the brochure?"

Susie's heart races. She feels her baby kick again, sharing her terror. Pat is there, waiting, suddenly alert for rebuff, ready to harden into a mask of offence.

"Oh Pat, I'd love to. Are you sure, though? I mean it's something so — private. Would Clinton mind?"

"If you don't mind, I don't."

Oh Jesus. Oh Jesus. She wants to see the Leonardo brochure. That's what this is about. She'll show me hers and I'll have to show her mine.

"Pat, it's a lovely idea, but I don't think I ought to see your brochure when I can't show you mine. You see, Reuben made me promise. I know it's silly, but he's so afraid something may go wrong. We haven't even shown it to our families."

Pat stares at her, her face without expression. "OK," she says. "It was just a thought." And she turns away and walks into her own house.

Jesus, Jesus, Jesus. She's offended. She's angry. She won't ever forget this. It's like offering to let someone see you naked and they say, "No thanks, I'm busy just now." She will never forgive me. Those brochures. Those fucking brochures. They've even made a ceremony of handing them over, sealed in transparent plastic coffins so they can never be taken out, or copied, or lent. It's the safest system outside the Bank of Zurich, and we couldn't break it.

It is getting towards the blue of evening when Reuben comes home.

"Let's eat in the garden. This is the best time of the day." He scans her face, watching for the symptoms neither of them have ever knowingly seen. The marks of a naturally conceived, naturally developing pregnancy. She has visited no antenatal clinic, Leonardo or Michelangelo or SuperStork, but they trust to the medical student. He examines her regularly, brings iron, vitamins, takes blood. They pay him what he asks, but the money isn't what matters to him. This is his mission. He tells them that there are other pregnancies like their own, covert, covertly assisted. Sometimes they're

39

discovered, but often they are not. Once, Susie asked him why he took such risks. "It's self-interest," he said. "If we don't protect human biodiversity, then in the end the species won't survive. And besides —" He looked at her, his hands on her stomach, and she looked back with the same anger, the same ferocious glee. Later, he will deliver the child in the back bedroom which they have spent weeks sound-proofing.

Susie clutches Reuben's arm. "No. Let's not go outside. Pat and Clinton are having a barbecue."

"Well, that doesn't stop us."

"No. Listen."

He listens, stilled, to the story of the brochures. She wants him to say that she's making too much of it, but he does not. He walks around the hot room, frowning. The air is thick and stale, and his shirt is pasted to his back.

"She's told Clinton about it," Susie goes on. "I've been listening at the back. And he said, 'That's strange. You know, Pat, I think that's strange. You'd think she'd want to share a thing like this.' And then Pat said, 'She said it was because of Reuben.' And he said, 'I don't believe that.'"

Susie and Reuben look at each other, and see the same fear and uncertainty reflected.

"I'm going out there," says Reuben. "It doesn't seem normal if we stay in on a night like this."

She hears his footsteps go across the little terrace. She feels the flood of air wash through the open door and around her body. It is scented with the honeysuckle, beguilingly, achingly sweet. Words come through the warm dusk.

"Wonderful evening. Your barbecue smells good."

"Yes." Is Susie imagining it, or is Clinton's voice different from usual? "Pat's feeling the heat. I expect Susie's the same."

"That's right."

"Heard the news tonight?"

"What? No, I didn't."

"Baby born with no arms in Birmingham."

"No, I didn't hear that. Well, I suppose they'll be suing their service."

"They didn't use any service. The mother's confessed, and they've arrested four accessories."

Reuben says nothing. His silence washes around Susie, like the evening air. *Say something*, she pleads without a sound. *Say they deserve it. Say how shocking it is*.

"She deserves it," intones Clinton. "It's criminal irresponsibility, that's what it is. Why should the rest of us pay for it?"

The question hangs, and is not answered.

"Well, I'll leave you to enjoy the rest of your evening. Looks like another hot day tomorrow," says Reuben.

Later, Susie and Reuben listen by their open window. In the next garden, the two voices are low. Lowered. They buzz, like a hive preparing to swarm.

In the middle of the night, Susie wakes. She does not know at first what has woken her. She turns over, the sheets sticking to her naked body. Then she hears it, the subdued tapping from downstairs that had got tangled in her dreams. Susie gets clumsily out of bed, goes to the

41

window, looks down, and there is Pat. Pat's upturned face wan with moonlight, Pat's body dwindling into shadow. Seeing Susie, she stops tapping at the back door, and beckons. Susie stumbles down through the hot, silent house. She opens the back door and Pat is there.

"Ssh. Listen." Pat's eyes are black, her face emptied of feature by the moonlight. "Clinton's going to ring the police tomorrow. He's going to ask them to run a check on you."

Susie says nothing.

"He's been suspicious for ages. Little things."

Susie moistens her lips. "Why —"

"I've got to go. Hush. Don't say anything."

And Pat melts backwards into the summer night, as if she has never been there. A few seconds later, there is the faintest of clicks as her door closes. Susie looks down, and realizes that she is naked.

* * *

In an hour, they are gone. They make no calls, take only a couple of bags. They don't even lock the doors. There's no point; they know the house will be eviscerated. The night is stifling. Thunder growls as they get into the car, and lightning dances in the distance. Soon there will be rain, sheets of it, covering their journey through the city, on to the motorway and then, later, off it again, down a slip road that narrows to a lane.

"Where are we?" asks Susie, waking. "I've got such a pain."

Rain drums on the roof of the car, and the wipers shovel plumes of water from side to side.

"Where?"

"My back. And I think I've wet myself."

"Oh Christ."

He slows into a gap by a farm gate, and peers through the windscreen.

"I've got to stand up," says Susie.

They walk through the rain, slowly, braced together, hair plastered to bowed heads. In his other hand Reuben carries a bag into which he has crammed baby clothes, towels, antiseptic, a torch.

"It's all right, Susie, we're nearly there. It's a barn."

He is wrong. The building is a disused pigsty, with a pile of sacks in the corner of its concrete floor.

"Scissors," gasps Susie after the next contraction. "Did you bring the scissors?"

"Yes."

The baby is born towards morning, after a fast, ferocious labour that terrifies Reuben. He blunders, he panics, he does everything wrong. He never thought there could be so much blood. He longs for it to end any way it has to, now, quickly, even if they are all left dead on the floor of the pigsty. But in spite of him, the baby is born. And there is Susie, with her own face again, looking at him. He has padded her against the flow of her blood, and thrown her placenta into the brimming ditch.

"Two arms," she says.

"I bet they all have two arms," he answers, wedging the child in close to her. "Lie still. I'll go and get the car ready. I'll put your seat right back, and we'll have the baby beside you, under the shawl."

"Why do you think she did it?" asks Susie. "Pat."

"I don't know."

"Thank God it's summer. Think if it'd been the middle of winter, having the baby in here."

Suddenly Susie is asleep. Reuben looks down at her. If they'd stayed, the baby would have been ripped from Susie and put into a hospital incinerator. *An outlaw conception has been destroyed*, they might have said on the local news. Sometimes, after a few such reports, there's a phone-in. An expert is always on hand to repeat that eugenic health demands constant vigilance. At the end, the services advertise. Leonardo, Michelangelo, SuperStork.

One phone call. He wonders if Clinton has made it yet.

The storm has quietened to summer rain, tapping the leaves. Water gurgles in the ditch. They must move on, even if it's to nowhere. Already, their baby has lived for an hour.

The Lighthouse Keeper's Wife

She'd gone. She hadn't waited for him.

Nancy always waited for him. She believed that there would always be a good reason if he was late. Not like his sister May. May thought disaster had come if she had to wait ten minutes for Jack to meet her outside the Stores. She'd look at her pocket-watch, glance up the street, shake her watch busily, as if it might not be working. May believed the worst, then drew it to herself. She'd had money since she married Jack, and she lived in town as she'd always wanted, but it made no difference.

He thought all those thoughts as he went up the stairs. There would have been time to live through a whole life while he climbed. He put his hand on the round curve of the plaster, as he always did. Its little prickling points were invisible to the eye, but he felt them. The door to the room was open and the room was full of sun. Fear prickled him, like the plaster. People had said Nancy would never stand the life, but she had stood it. She was everything he was not, light and graceful, laughing out of a crowd. She would stand with her sisters at the street corner, her skirts blowing, her face whipped with laughter. No one else could dream of belonging in that tight circle.

He loved to watch her. He would rather watch Nancy dancing than dance himself. He would sit very upright, his eyes sharp and distant, his body planted in the chair so that little by little the room felt its presence, and the girls would glance at him as they went by.

They said she would never stand the loneliness of the life, with him gone for his twenty-eight days' duty six times a year. He had moved her ten miles down the coast from her sisters. She'd slept with them every night of her life, she told him. Nancy and Liza together, Hester in the buckle, then Sarey in her cot-bed behind the door. She'd stared round their bedroom the first night they were married, and then she'd taken a run and a jump and landed in the middle of their big bed and let herself fall back with her arms wide, feeling all that space, laughing.

The bed was too big when she lay alone in it. He was an off-shore lighthouseman and she knew that when she married him. If the lighthouse tender couldn't land to change crew on relief day, Nancy might be waiting for him another week. Often the weather was bad when it came to changeover. He'd watch the wall of white foam crash against the glass and know he wasn't going to get off. But Nancy stood it. She had her little garden. She didn't flinch. She knew all the fishing boats and would stand to watch them go out around the point, her skirts blown back against her legs, moulded to them by the wind. He was glad there was no one else to see her like that. She fed her garden with fish-meal and rotted-down seaweed, and when salt-storms burnt off the leaves of her spinach and lettuces, she planted again. He would see her kneeling on the path, skirts bunched under her, tamping the seedlings in with her quick fingers.

Sometimes she would walk the ten miles to Carrack Cross to see her sisters, but she would never stay more than one night. When he asked her why, she shrugged and said, "This is my life now." He would watch her scrambling over the black, sharp rocks, picking mussels at low tide with her skirts kilted up. If she climbed the cliff he knew she could look westward as far as the grey tumble of houses that was Carrack Cross. When she set off with her basket to pick blackberries or early mushrooms, he had to fight the fear that she would never come home again, and that the prints of her stout black boots on the wet fields would be the last thing he would ever see of her.

Slowly, methodically, he would climb the lighthouse tower, towards the light, thinking of her. A mound of sea thudded against the tower, then fell back and weaselled at the foot of the rock, getting its strength. Nancy said she did not mind thinking of him in the lighthouse, no matter how bad the storms, but what she kept out of her thoughts was the moment when he was brought off the landing-platform, with the sea hungry for him and the lighthouse tender pitching. Sometimes the sight of it came into her mind at night, before she could push it away. It made her sick to think of it, she said, though he knew she could walk to the edge of the cliff and stand there without a moment's dizziness.

He was standing still, not on the steps of the lighthouse tower, but on his own staircase, at home, one hand on the plaster wall. He must go on up to her, where she was waiting for him.

She was there, as he'd known she would be. Her toes pointed up through the sheets and she looked like a child waiting to be kissed goodnight. They'd often thought of when Michael would be old enough to talk to them and have a story at bedtime. Would they teach him to say his night prayers? Nancy thought yes, Blaise no. He knew she already said a prayer over Michael when she put him in his cot. He had no faith in it himself, but believed there was no harm, if Nancy did it.

He stood in the doorway and stared at her toes, because he was afraid to follow the white sweep of her body up to her face. He had seen terrible things done to the faces of the dead, when the sea got them. Nothing must touch her eyebrows that flexed like two fine black wings when she laughed. Nothing must touch her mouth. He'd noticed her mouth before he noticed anything else about her.

The sunlight was strong. It made him blink. But those windows were dirty. It made you realize what had been blowing on to them all winter. All that salt. It had made a crust on the panes. He would clean them for her. She'd lain there and listened to the rain, all night long sometimes. She never told him that she lay awake, but he knew it from the way the skin under her eyes was dry and sunk with sleeplessness. It had been a dark, long winter, but now it was over.

"Winter's over." She'd said that yesterday, hearing a scuffle of starlings in the roof-space. He'd wondered if he should smoke out the birds for her. Starlings were filthy things, full of mites. And then she'd said the sun was reaching higher on the wall opposite her bed.

"Look, it's up to that mark on the plaster now."

She'd pointed. This was a world of her own, in this room. The rest had shrunk away from her, and she no longer asked about it, or even noticed the wood-anemones and celandines her sisters brought her, their stems packed into wet moss. The baby sounded far off, though he was only downstairs. These past two weeks she'd stopped asking for Michael. She couldn't hold him any more. Michael was too strong for her. He kicked, and she cried out. It was just weakness, she said, her lips white.

He'd unlaced his boots at the top of the stairs, ready. Now he took them off so there'd be no noise to trouble her. He went over to Nancy and touched her feet. The darn on the counterpane ran up the side of the little tent her body made. She had darned that darn. It was her own fine stitching. He might have watched her do it, but when? Suddenly he saw her, sitting opposite him through the evenings of his off-duty, her polished head moving just a little with each stab of her needle. She didn't look up. Didn't look at him.

He had his hand round her feet, holding them tight. Why hadn't they flopped to one side as they did when she relaxed into sleep? When she was deep into her sleep she seemed boneless. She turned away from him, one fist up to her face, dreaming into it.

The bottom stair creaked. Someone coming. There'd been people all the time since they sent Nancy home from the hospital, not able to do any more for her. Her sisters most of all. He put out his hand to fend them off but the next stair creaked, and the next. Someone was walking up, slowly, steadily. As quick as thought he crossed to the door and shut it. There was no bolt, just the latch. No key he could turn. He called out in a voice that was unfamiliar to him. "Wait. I'll be down."

There was no answer. Whoever it was stood still, then creaked away, heavily. Maybe it was the doctor. He flushed, alone behind the door, because of his incivility. The doctor was old. He knew Nancy. He didn't whisk in and out, he sat with her. He never left her without making sure that she would be able to hold down the pain until his next visit. You could never pay enough for treatment like that. Blaise would not let her suffer like they'd let her suffer on the ward. He had used up all the money Nancy'd begun to set aside for Michael when she first knew she was pregnant.

All his thoughts turned in him like a cloud of gulls, disturbed. He couldn't bear to let them settle. What if he looked at her again? Which way had they turned her head? Or did it lie as she had turned it?

She was lying with her face toward the window. He almost laughed in relief. After all his thinking, it was easy enough to look at her. What was she doing turned that way, instead of facing the door as she always did when she heard his tread on the stairs? He could see her now, up on her elbows in her white nightgown, with a rosy bruise of sleep on her face where she'd crushed it into the pillow.

But she was turned to the window. Maybe she didn't expect him. She couldn't hear how still the air was, or see how calm the water lay in the bay. In her dreams she thought he was still out at the lighthouse, waiting for the storm to be over so that he could be taken off. When the sea was calm she would always be there to meet him, on the exact day, at the exact hour. She'd have Michael on her hip, shading his eyes against the sun.

A noise burst from his throat. He stumbled back across the floor to her, and knelt at the side of her bed. Her hands were smooth at her sides, outside the bedclothes. Her face was white, but no paler than she'd been many other days. Nancy'd never had much colour even before she was ill. Her hair was a bit untidy on her forehead. So close, he could see tiny grey strands in it. He'd never noticed them before. She was only twenty-nine. In her family they went grey young, but it looked right on them, even youthful. All her sisters had those clear faces and large, beautiful eyes, but he couldn't see the beauty in any of them except her. It was strange to see them in ranks, staring out at you from a photograph. It made Nancy look less herself.

Her eyes were shut. Of course they would be. But he'd seen this closure before. This sunkenness, a gap left by something suddenly gone. Her lids didn't lie lightly over her eyes, cushioned by flowing blood. They seemed to stick to the round globes of her eyeballs. He put out a hand, but against her face it only showed how she had no colour, none at all. He cupped the side of her face. She's not cold, he thought triumphantly. Not cold at all. Let them get out of that. He glanced behind him but there was no one there. His breath came lumpily, as if he'd been running. He'd been a good runner, a fine runner once. No use now. She'd seen him pass them all in the men's eight-hundred-yard dash. She'd smiled then. Let them dare say that she was cold.

He felt her again. He snuggled her face against his hand. There was his thumb against her cheek. His thumb looked dirty, though he always scrubbed his hands before he came up to her. He was afraid of the way she felt now. Always before when he'd touched her, he'd believed he could feel her blood moving. Her blood ran faster and more brightly than other people's, and closer to the surface of her skin. She had bled a lot when Michael was born. They'd had to throw the mattress away, even though she'd wadded it with newspaper under her. Maybe she was ill then, before they knew it. Nancy might be pale but her fingers were warm in the coldest winter, and she never needed to wear gloves. Sometimes she'd put her hand in his pocket, while they were walking.

Her body lay like a basin of cooling water, neither cold nor hot. He bent over as if to kiss her cheek, but he did not touch her. He was afraid to make a dent in her flesh and see it stay there. Her lips were slightly parted and there was a bubble of saliva on the corner of her mouth. If she'd known it she'd have knocked it away quickly, before he saw it, with the back of her hand.

"Nancy," he said, quietly, not to embarrass her, the way he'd once pointed out wordlessly that she had a splotch of blood on the back of her pink summer skirt. But she lay still.

From downstairs he heard the noise of a baby crying. Angry, frustrated crying. He listened for a minute before he realized that it was Michael. He'd have been trying to get into the cupboards again. He liked to bang the cups together and smash them. If Nancy'd been downstairs the baby wouldn't have cried. He remembered suddenly how he'd been in the kitchen once when Michael tried to stand against a kitchen chair, then he'd slipped and knocked the corner of his eye as he came down on to the floor. A splash of the baby's blood hit the cardinal-red tiles. It was only a little cut but it was deep. Before the baby knew he was hurt Nancy had swooped down and picked him up. In a minute he was smiling, with a clean white handkerchief pressed over his eye. The cut stopped bleeding almost at once, but it left a mark, a thin white line over the eye. That mark was there now.

Downstairs the crying rose to a pitch. The baby would be bucking in the arms of the sister who was holding him, straining his head back and screaming, his face patched red with rage. Then he'd close in and bite, then cry again, frightened at what he'd done. He never used to be like this. Only since Nancy went away to the hospital.

"My wife," he said aloud, staring at Nancy. It seemed a long time since he had said those words. They were as awkward now as they'd been those weeks after the wedding, when he'd had to shape his lips to it before he could say "my wife" with an air of ease. And then from one day to the next he'd got used to it, and stopped saying it. He called her Nancy sometimes, but mostly "you". He'd said to her this morning, "Will you be all right? I'm going now, to fetch you the Bengers Food."

53

She needed building up. She could not take solid food, and that was what was weakening her. He had ordered the Bengers Food for her, and it would be delivered by Trelawny's cart, as far as New Hayle farm. It was only three miles to walk. He would be back before she knew it.

And she'd said "Yes", without smiling, not seeming to pay much attention to him or what was said. He knew she was dull from the stuff the doctor had given her. He hated it, but he knew it was better for her that way. So that was it, he thought now in amazement. That was her last word to me. That flat "Yes", about nothing at all.

Ice Cream

It is just before midnight on Clara's twenty-fourth birthday when she begins to think of ice cream.

"Clara! Clara, darling. Coffee?"

And just as Clara opens her beautiful mouth to let out the automatic murmur of "double espresso", a heaped, glistening plate of ice cream glides past her on its way to a woman at the next table. Clara never eats ice cream. Not even this celebrated vanilla, grained like raw silk, pure yet wicked. She does not even think of eating ice cream, any more than she thinks of committing murder or lying in the midday sun.

"*Clara.* I've ordered a double espresso for you. Wake up, sweetie."

But Clara cannot wake up. The theatre of the restaurant is stilled, silent. The black-clad waiters and waitresses arch over their tables, frozen. She hears nothing and sees nothing. The scent of vanilla curls into her nostrils, the unctuousness of cream ravishes her tongue. Clara licks her lips. She clears her throat.

"I think I — I think I'll —"

The waiter snaps a perfect cup of espresso down in front of her, and smiles. Trained though he is, cool though he wishes to be, he finds himself smiling at Clara.

There is something about her beauty which compels it. Her beauty is warm, not cold. She is as tantalizing as the geography of Tahiti. But Clara does not smile back. The buzz of her birthday party continues around her, glasses lift and fall, faces grow flushed above the wreck of the table, expensive bodies sheathed in expensive clothes twist this way and that. And all for Clara, whose fame is surely at its height, because there are no more peaks left for her to climb. But it is impossible to imagine her fading. She will stay there for ever, at her zenith, her lovely eyes as remote and seductive as they were when they first looked into a lens.

"*Ice cream,*" whispers Clara, and her voice cracks. Elise, Clara's personal trainer, is sitting halfway down the table, but her greyhound ears pick up the forbidden word. Excusing herself, she stands and eels her way around the table until she is behind Clara's chair.

"Close your eyes, Clara. Deep breaths. You are lying on golden sand, Clara, by the blue ocean. Listen to the waves. Listen to the wind in the palm trees. You are completely relaxed, completely relaxed . . ."

The litany hums into Clara's head as it has done a thousand times before. She hears the waves, sees them break, watches the foam crash up the shore, as cool and white as —

"Ice cream," says Clara again, opening her eyes. The waiter hovers, looking from Clara to Elise. They are beginning to attract attention.

"Clara," insists Elise. "Remember."

Clara remembers. Elise knows things nobody else knows. She knows about a huge golden-skinned fourteen-year-old Clara, as wide and sleek as a whale. She knows about a fridge stacked with ginger ice cream, apricot ice cream, coffee ice cream the colour of the palest tan, the burnt taste of it made mellifluous by sugar and cream. Elise knows about Belgian chocolate and ice cream perfumed with fragile wood-strawberries, crushed by hand into bowlfuls of thick, cool, yellow cream. Elise can make Clara remember how beauty does not exist of itself, but has to be carved out of flesh. It is a thing of bones and shadows. When Elise's voice whispers in Clara's ear, Clara remembers her early days, tramping from agency to agency, in the hope that one might put her on their books. Clara had no money for taxis then. She went into glossy lobbies that smelled of stephanotis, and she toiled up bare wooden staircases that smelled of yesterday's curry. She still feels the burn of experienced, indifferent eyes travelling over her body, her skin, her hair.

"Come back when you've lost two stone."

And Clara did it. She knows she would never have done it without Elise, who saw her potential before anyone else did. Clara came back, risen from her flesh like Venus.

"Remember, Clara," says Elise.

"Oh Christ," says Julie opposite, crushing out her cigarette in a meringue shell. "Is she getting at you again?" Her Slavic cheekbones lift in a grimace. "If you're that desperate, why don't you do what everybody else does?" And delicately, elegantly, she mimes the hook of a forefinger down a throat. Up and down the table the ripple of interest grows. Sympathetic, professional, Clara's colleagues address themselves to the problem.

"I've got some fabulous pills," confides Tanya in her East-end aristo drawl, snaking across her boyfriend to peer into Clara's face. "I don't know what they are but they simply *kill* the pangs. But better not take them all the time, darling. Just for a couple of days before a shoot."

"Speed kills, *darling*," growls pale, frail Charlotte, who still maintains to all comers that she is "naturally thin". But Elise kneads her fingers deep into Clara's shoulder.

"Mouth therapy," she pronounces. "That is what you need, Clara." The stir of interest up and down the table is more than a ripple now. Like a wave, photographers, actors, agents, editors lean forward to catch what Elise has to offer to Clara. Elise is at the cutting edge. To be personally trained by Elise you have to have more than money. And Clara, golden Clara, is the jewel in Elise's crown.

"What you think is hunger is not real hunger," says Elise. She is still kneading at Clara's flesh, and her voice has dropped to a sing-song. "It's only mouth hunger. So *satisfy* that hunger. Fill your mouth. Let your mouth have the pleasure it wants. Then — discard it. Let it go."

Tanya, who is not very clever, looks puzzled. But Julie has caught on.

"Spit it out again, she means."

"Spit it out."

"Spit it out."

The words run up and down the table, catching on. *Mouth therapy*. How remarkable. And how amazing that no one has thought of it before. None of them notices how the waiter has stiffened, how he frowns. But Clara looks up at him as a drowning woman looks her last at land. Her mouth moves. "Ice cream," she murmurs.

"Oh no," says Elise briskly. "Mouth therapy won't work with ice cream. It's too —"

"Creamy," says Clara, and her mouth widens into a smile. She holds the waiter's gaze until he feels as if he too is drowning, in the rare and lovely oceans of Tahiti. Then he bows his head, and spins round on his heel, towards the kitchen. Clara looks down, her head softly bent, waiting, while Elise expounds her theory to the entire table. Everyone listens, so absorbed that they do not see the waiter return, bearing a platter triumphantly aloft in one hand.

Then there is a breath of wood-strawberries, a burnt aroma of coffee, the silk-sweet innocence of vanilla, the spice of ginger, the ice-green tang of lime. The waiter lowers his platter to the table and places it before Clara.

"No!" cries Elise. "Remember, Clara!"

But Clara remembers nothing. She lifts her spoon. Its silver edge cuts into the creamy pallor of vanilla. She lifts the spoon to her mouth, opens her lips. The waiter's lips move too, encouraging her as a mother encourages her baby to eat. Clara puts the ice cream in her mouth. It softens on her palate and her tongue, and Clara half-closes her eyes, so intense is the bliss of sweetness and ice. She has never looked so beautiful, so meltingly seductive as she does now, as Elise turns away in sorrow, and Clara, Clara . . .

Clara swallows.

Be Vigilant, Rejoice, Eat Plenty

You didn't realize they'd put those new parking meters along here. Not the old-fashioned meters, one for each car, which sometimes break down and let you park free. The new ones, righteous as policemen under totalitarian regimes. They have a display which tells you what to do, and what will happen if you don't do it. They know what your time is worth.

You count out the twenty-pence pieces. Ten minutes for the bank, another five to get to the coffee shop, half an hour to have the argument with Max, ten minutes to walk back. You'll need an hour at least. More, to be safe. You've never forgotten the moment when you came dreamily out of the toyshop, clutching the baby as if you'd just bought him there, and saw the towaway truck backing on to your car.

They let you off. Didn't take the car, but you still had the fine slapped across the window. So now you tap in your registration number, and feed the machine your twenty-pence pieces. The sun's so bright you have to shade the display panel with your hands and peer in to be sure that the computer has got it right. 11.26, it says.

Then: BE VIGILANT. The message flicks off. You peer again. It's like trying to catch your bank balance on the screen when you take money out from the hole in the wall. Now the machine seems frozen. No figures on it, none of the computerized chuntering that lets you know it's digested your information and is processing your ticket. Nothing. You find another twenty pence. Feed it in. The display panel looks you straight in the eye. REJOICE, it says.

Now you are determined. You don't care how much this conversation costs, you're going to have it in full. You shove in a pound coin. EAT PLENTY, says the machine. The message stays on-screen a little longer than before, then disappears.

There's no more money in your purse. You rummage in the lining of your handbag, but find only a paracetamol tablet. You look around. There is no one in the street, so you lean forward and speak straight into the display.

"Cheat. That wasn't a pound's worth."

The digitized figures whirr round, and are replaced by words. The same words, floating by so quickly you are not sure whether you caught them or not.

"BE VIGILANT. REJOICE. EAT PLENTY."

The sun is warm on your back. How long is it since you felt that? Last October, maybe. The street is full of the prickly whites and yellows of spring. What have you come here for? For a minute you can't remember.

Bank. Argue with Max. Back to the childminder's. This is your time, time you've paid for doubly. Paid the childminder, paid the parking machine.

You could do anything. Look at that man coming down the street, snail-like between two sticks, bent. He stops, lifts up his face to the sun, closes his eyes. For a long moment he stays there. Above him there is plum blossom, tentatively opening on its black twigs and branches.

You step away from the machine, since it seems to have nothing more to say to you. You walk quietly. These are your minutes. You could be arguing with Max: in fact you've got to argue with Max. About money, of course. You've been too civilized to go to court, or let the CSA in on your affairs. He doesn't give you enough, and the less he gives, the more he hates you for making him know how mean he is.

"All right, all right," he says each time, weary, civilized. "I'll write a cheque." And he writes one, in his beautiful creamy chequebook, with his Mont Blanc pen. When you say you have to get back now, because of the childminder, he says that he doesn't see the point of you working. After all, it scarcely pays, does it, once you've paid the childminder? You don't seem able to manage on it.

You've never walked down this street so slowly. And the wonderful thing comes to you suddenly. It's not reluctance to meet Max. It's because you like it like this. Those new paving-stones, so beautifully fitted together. The man who's finishing off the last bit of paving, who wedges in a stone and, considering it, looks up and catches your eye. And smiles. What beautiful eyes he has. Pure blue in his battered face. Then a pigeon begins to coo on the branch of a magnolia above your head, and you look up and see it isn't a pigeon at all, but a dove. Fancy someone keeping doves round here, in all the traffic. But it has the sense to keep safe, up there in the magnolia which is almost fully open now.

A girl hurries uphill and passes you. She has a carrier bag in each hand and the reason she's hurrying, you know it, is that she's just bought the most amazing new dress and she can't wait to try it on at home, because it's never the same in shops. The mirrors don't know you. And the shoes, too; she bought the shoes. She is beautiful. Warm and eager, the kind of beauty that spills over itself and doesn't care that one day it'll all be gone.

"Why don't you go to a health club?" says Max. "Why don't you get yourself some decent clothes? Surely you have enough money?"

You have enough. You think of the baby, who is three now. He looks like Max. He is not like Max. When he sees you unexpectedly, when you are early at the childminder's, for example, and she has not prepared him for your return, you sometimes get a moment to watch him. And then he looks up and sees you and his smile, amazed, incredulous, radiant, blooms all over his face as if he has just invented you for the first time.

Just there, down the hill, is the coffee shop. And there, coming out of it into the spring light, is Max. He squints up and down the street, but does not see you. You see again how handsome he is in his dark-grey suit. He won't wait for you, because his time is money. You watch as he sets off smartly down the hill, to where he will have parked his car in the car park which is slightly cheaper than the metered side streets. He begins to mingle with other people, going up and down the hill. You lose him, and you can't find him again. He's gone, with his chequebook snug in his inner pocket, and his pen still capped.

You walk into the coffee shop. You do not stop at one of the spindly tables where you would have sat with Max, one at each side, wary and uncomfortable. He would have ordered espresso for both of you, without asking. This is what you always drink.

You go upstairs, to the smoking room, where there are sofas and armchairs. You sit down. All around you are tables full of people. You listen, and you hear what they cannot yet hear. It's a sound which they will stop being able to make as soon as they know what it is. It is just the sound of being young.

You remember that you have to order downstairs. You go to the counter and order hot chocolate, with whipped cream and cinnamon. As you speak, a tray is carried past you: a baker's tray, loaded with croissants and brioches. From the smell, you know they are still warm. They are plump, moist, golden. You point to the tray.

"I'll have two croissants," you say. "And one of those brioches as well."

"With cherry jam, or apricot?"

"Both," you say.

The girl behind the counter smiles, like a comrade encountered far behind enemy lines. "Both," she confirms.

You are walking back upstairs, with your wooden tray. You look at your watch and see that you have fifty minutes left. Your own minutes, which belong to you doubly now that Max has left. He might have been here, and he is not. He might have been uncapping his pen at this moment, striking the first black line across the cream of his cheque.

You sit down. You watch a little girl with her father, enchanted by a man on a stepladder changing a light-bulb. You think of your little boy, not with you, but safe. If Max was here you wouldn't let him write in his chequebook. You would say, *We have been civilized long enough.*

BE VIGILANT, you think. REJOICE. EAT PLENTY. You raise the buttery nub of the croissant to your lips.

The Clear and Rolling Water

The land was lichen coloured, and the water ran through it fast and clear, rolling the stones with it a little way and then letting them fall. I never thought about the colours of the hills, or the way the river flowed, as long as I lived there. They were there each morning when I opened the door: a fresh, cold shock of light and river noise. I would remember that the river had been there all the time, even in my dreams. I didn't know how to go to sleep without it, the rushing sound of it as faint as my own blood in my eyes. When the snow melted and the river rose high you would think you heard the boulders grinding one another, deep down under the water.

We had the land one side of the river, and the Robertsons had the land on the other, right down to the water. That was how it had always been, and it would have been so for ever if my father hadn't decided to get out of sheep. The prices had fallen so far it was scarcely worth the petrol to take them to market. And besides, he was sick of them. He had always wanted more out of life than the sheep and the river and the high hills where the sheep strayed and lost themselves and were prey to foxes and crows. He had never thought this would be all his life would add up to.

"What more?" my mother said. "What more do you want?" I remember this. I was listening because I was waiting for Jamie, and had nothing better to do. We were going up the river, to fish a little, maybe, and then build a fire with flat stones in a ring. I had my mother's biggest baking potatoes deep in the pockets of my anorak. But I must have stopped listening then, because I don't remember what my father answered. He went out to fix slates on the tractor-shed roof before Jamie knocked at the door.

Jamie was twelve then, and I would soon be eleven. We were the only children for three miles, dropped off by the school bus together at the lane-end on Friday afternoons. We could have seen other kids if we'd wanted to: three miles wasn't so far. Usually we didn't want anything but the silence of walking with just ourselves, and the noise of the school bus fading from our heads. Jamie was already at the High School, and I would go next year. He knew the names of big girls with breasts and flouncing hair who smoked at the back of the bus. I knew I knew nothing. I couldn't believe that next year would find me there, wearing the navy uniform instead of my primary-school sweatshirt. I looked at my thin chest in the bath and despaired that breasts would ever grow there.

Sometimes we walked on one side of the river, sometimes on the other. We rarely thought about it being Robertson land or Foster land. Anyway, we were soon beyond what either family owned, where the river ran more steeply, pummelling the boulders where we climbed and jumped and balanced. It was best to stay close to the river once we got high up the valley, because the land on either bank was uncultivated, full of bracken and furze and flies. By the water's edge there were young rowans, which dropped their berries in the water each autumn. It was here, once, that we thought we saw a wildcat, moulded to the lip of a rock, staring down at us with blank yellow eyes. But we knew there were no wildcats any more.

We picked wild raspberries, and bilberries. We knew the best places and we never took so much as a berry home. We gobbled them all out of our juice-stained hands, crushing them into our juice-stained mouths. Often we found sheep bones, and skulls where you could see the fit of the bone, piece to piece, like fine seaming. If it was a ram's skull we might keep it.

Even when the water was high and dangerous we still jumped from boulder to boulder. We must have slipped often, but I remember one time when I leaped and knew halfway that I'd misjudged it and would fall into the thrash of the water. But I hurled myself forward and caught at the side of the rock where it jutted. I knocked my breath out but I clung to the slippery side, sprawled across the face of the rock like a monkey, grappling it to me. Jamie hauled me up. I was on top of the rock and safe before I felt the blow the rock had given me.

In some parts the river had elbowed out backwater pools for itself. There was one pool where it was deep enough to swim, cold and deep. We would pull off our clothes and dry ourselves afterwards on handfuls of grass. I think there was a time when we swam naked, when we were just old enough to be let out to wander, but not old enough to care what we looked like. But by the time I was eleven I would wear my swimming costume under my clothes, and pull my jeans and T-shirt over my nakedness afterwards. There was no smell on your skin after swimming in the river, not like the chlorine taste when I licked my arm after school swimming lessons.

Then it was time for me to go to the High School. My parents gave me a fountain pen, in a presentation box lined with cream satin. They had money just then, because my father had taken out a loan to convert two of our outbuildings into holiday cottages. That was where the money was, he told us. People wanted peace and quiet, didn't they? They could walk up the river, or fish, or climb the hills. What if we were remote? Even town people had Landrovers these days. He would do most of the conversion himself, and my mother would make the curtains, and covers for the armchairs he'd buy cheap in sale rooms. He sat at the kitchen table, working out the rents. Visitors could come at Christmas, too, he reckoned. What could be better than Christmas away from it all, with no shops for miles, and the sound of the river instead of traffic? Two cottages to begin with, and then if it went well he would build log cabins on the land lower down, towards the river. Maybe schools would bring kids up here on camp.

"Not with the river," my mother said. "They'd have to have eyes in the backs of their heads, watching twenty or thirty children."

"What harm's ever come to Laura from the river?"

"I know," said my mother, but as if she was talking to me, not to my father. He didn't seem to hear her anyway. He was too busy with figures, measuring and calculating. One day they went into town together, to talk to the bank.

So I had my fountain pen. I was getting taller, but not tall enough, and my new uniform hung on me. I looked in the mirror and looked quickly away, but my mother framed my face with her hands and kissed me.

"Have you got your fountain pen?"

"Yes."

Jamie waited for me by the bridge, and we walked up the track together, as usual. I thought suddenly how much he had grown in the summer. He was nearly thirteen, and going into the second year. My new bag bumped on my back, and Jamie told me lots of things about school, quickly, as if we'd never talked about it before. I thought of my pen in my bag, inside its case.

It was Isobel Farmer who took my pen. She held it high above her head, jeering. "Ooh, Laurer Foster."

The satin lining fell out of the box and the pen shone in Isobel's big hand. She snatched a piece of paper, uncapped my pen, and began to write, pressing down hard. Ink spattered as the nib crossed. Isobel threw down the pen. "Your mum bought it off a tinker, that's why it doesn't write. They don't have shops where Laura lives."

I didn't tell Jamie. It was my first calculation concerning him: before that I'd told him my thoughts as soon as I had them. But I didn't want him to fight Isobel

Farmer for me. I would do it myself, when I had worked out how it could be done. When I got home no one was thinking about pens, because Dad had got his loan and all the plans were going ahead. It was like Christmas, coming terrifyingly fast.

No one expects a business to make money in the first year. Dad said that often, and I believed it. The cottages were an investment which would pay for themselves many times over. They had to have kitchenettes, and showers, and everything people would want when they were on holiday. My mother made everything she could, to save money, and my father worked on the buildings until the long summer light faded. He did the electrics himself, and all the plastering. The painting was easy: Jamie and I rollered the bedroom walls. When the cottages were finished we were proud of them, and besides, I thought, how could the visitors fail to love the river, the grey stones where you could sit and fish, and the narrow paths through the bracken up on to the hills. My mother had already advertised the cottages, and calls were coming in.

It didn't fail at once, quickly. Maybe it would have been less cruel if it had done so. Visitors came, but only for a week, and then there would be a gap of a fortnight, and perhaps a cancellation. They would say that they had enjoyed themselves, but they didn't come back. No one booked for Christmas, or Easter, or New Year. In summer they asked if we could put screens over the windows, against the midges. My mother advertised in walking magazines, and magazines for painters. I came to dread the arrival of the visitors, and their polite faces when my mother showed them round. I knew that a day or two later I would see them standing outside the cottage door, staring at the river, the sheep, the hills, the curtain of cloud whose softness I loved. Their faces would ask: is this all there is? My mother put tubs of marigolds and daisies outside the cottage doors, and collected tourist leaflets for a file. She said I would take them on guided walks. In the evenings she and my father made calculations on pieces of paper.

The third summer, my mother no longer planted the tubs. I was fifteen. Jamie said, "We'll go swimming. We'll go all day tomorrow." He knew how much I wanted to get away from the cottages. It was the day my parents had to go and see the bank again, and I was supposed to stay by the telephone in case there were bookings. But I knew there wouldn't be.

We went up the river. It was warm, but it was mid-August and you could already feel the autumn coming. The rowan berries were red, the bracken was beginning to bronze. I thought of the winter coming, which I used to love, and of how my parents had said that this winter it was not worth repainting the cottages. We reached the pool. I was still thin, but I was tall now and I had at last got the breasts I'd feared I'd never get. Not round, squashy breasts like the girls at the back of the bus, who'd long since left school, but enough. Isobel Farmer was pregnant and I was glad of it when the boys said she was a slut and a slag and a dirty ride. There had been no need to fight her after all.

We took off our clothes. I had my black school swimming costume on underneath, and this time we had brought towels in our backpacks, as well as our sandwiches and crisps. But I didn't feel like swimming. I sat on a boulder, trailing my legs in the water, watching Jamie. He was a good swimmer and he loved diving and doing somersaults underwater. The water looked brown, but it was clear and I could see the paleness of his limbs, flicking and twisting in it. Then his head rose, round and brown. He pushed his hair back with both hands, treading water, smiling at me as the drops ran down his face.

He was cold when he came to sit beside me. He touched me and we laughed, then I rubbed his back hard with the towel, as I always did. The Robertson towels were thick and soft.

"When I'm old," he said, staring across the pool, "this is what I'll remember. Coming here. I'll be able to shut my eyes and see it, just as if it was still in front of me."

I was too frightened to look at him. I knew that he meant he was planning to leave, and the river was sliding into his past. He'd never said it so clearly before.

"I'll always come here," I said.

"No, you won't. You'll go away. You'll have to."

The sun was already slipping off the rocks. Jamie said, "I'm cold. Let's get dressed."

When we were dressed, Jamie said, "I've got to tell you something. My father wants to buy your father's grazing, by the river."

"He can't do that. My father wouldn't sell the land."

"He may have to. It would repay the loans."

The words would have sounded unkind if they hadn't been Jamie's. They burned me, because they were the

73

truths which haunted our house and could never be spoken. My father had failed. He had put all his hope and money into the cottages, and lost.

"My father has just written to yours, making an offer," said Jamie.

"But that means the river will be his. He'll have the land on both banks."

"Yes."

My father said he would never sell the land. He walked over the bridge and up to the Robertsons' farmhouse and put their letter back through their door. He didn't know that my mother telephoned Jessie Robertson and spoke to her for a long time in a voice which was too low for me to make out the words.

The bank wrote again. They wanted a new schedule for the repayment of the debt. They reminded my parents that the house and the land had been collateral for the loan.

"If I have to lose the land, it'll be to the bank, not to him."

My mother talked again, long and low, and this time I caught some of it. Robertson would give a good price for the land, but the bank would knock it down at auction and we'd end up losing our land without repaying our debts. Even if we sold it, we would still have the house, and the cottages, and the land behind us, up to the hills.

"And watch him walking up and down the riverbank in front of me," said my father.

The day the land was sold my father walked up the river into the hills and did not come back until dark. When he did he sat at the table, empty-eyed, and took no notice of the glass my mother put in front of him.

"They've got what they wanted," he said to me. "But if I see one of them put a foot beyond the land they've stolen, I'll get my shotgun."

He came to believe they had stolen it. My mother told me he was ill, and the doctor had given him pills which he wouldn't take. The loan was paid, and the long stretch of grazing which ran along the river had gone. My father watched as Robertson's men knocked in posts and strung barbed wire to mark the new boundary. The cottages stood empty. Who would come, if they could not even walk down to the river? Who would want to look out of their bedroom windows at the barbed wire? We would get sheep again, my mother said. We'd start in a small way, and prices were better now. There was nothing my father didn't know about sheep. We would do well.

"Don't let me see you with that Robertson boy again," said my father.

"She has to get the school bus," my mother observed.

"I'm warning you, Laura. Tell him not to put a foot on my land."

I told Jamie, but I'm not sure that he took it seriously. He was too busy thinking of exams and university entrance. He had all the university brochures and he brought them to show me the different courses. We sat together on the school bus, and I looked at the glossy photographs of students in bars, or sitting at ranks of computers, or browsing in libraries. I thought of the narrow track pelleted with sheep dung, and the barbed wire, and the river.

"You're really going," I said.

"Yes, and you will too."

"Will I?"

He smiled as if there were nothing more sure. It was summer again, almost time for the holidays. We would soon be back at the pool, and that was all I let myself think about. I never went to the Robertsons' any more, and Jamie never came up the track to our house.

Jamie was teaching me to dive. I'd always been nervous of it. There was something about hitting the water head-first that I didn't like, though I could jump from any height.

"Put your feet together and spring," Jamie told me. I put my feet together, curled them over the edge of the rock, swung up my arms, looked down. My feet were wet, the rock was slippery. It would have been fine if I hadn't looked down. I banged myself against the side of the rock as I fell and then I was in the water, half-stunned.

Jamie got me out. I saw his face, frightened, though I'd only fallen in the water as we'd often done.

"Your head," he said. "Your fucking head, Laura."

I'd gashed the side of my head as I came down. I couldn't see it, but when I put up my hand I felt the blood. Jamie grabbed his towel and pressed it hard against the side of my head. I was feeling strange and beginning to shiver, but Jamie was already wrapping my own towel around me.

"It's coming through," he said. "You're bleeding a lot. I'll have to go and get help."

We were a couple of miles above the houses.

"I'll run," he said. "I'll be quick. Press hard as you can now, Laura." He helped me peel off my swimsuit and pull on my shorts and a sweatshirt. He wrapped his own sweatshirt around my legs.

"I won't be long," he said. "It's bleeding less."

I felt the wetness and knew he was lying. But I wasn't frightened, although I felt sick and dizzy. I knew scalp wounds always bled. I was angry with myself for being so stupid, diving without having the courage to really dive.

I listened to his footsteps go away, crashing through the bracken. I thought that when Jamie peeled the black swimsuit off my body, it was the first time he had seen me naked since we were children. Soon silence thickened round me, with glints of flies drawn to my blood.

My father didn't come, nor did Jamie. When my father saw Jamie coming, running down the land on our side of the barbed wire, he went for his gun. When he shot Jamie he said he aimed low, for the legs, the way you do with poachers. But he wasn't so great a shot, and Jamie was running. He caught Jamie in the face and Jamie lost an eye. It was my mother who ran down and got to Jamie, lying on our side of the barbed wire. He told her where I was.

My father didn't go to prison, because of what the doctor told the court about his depression, and the pills, and the way he had an obsession that the Robertsons had stolen the land. And they must have believed my father when he said he had aimed low. But I'm not sure that I do. He's still having treatment.

So is Jamie. He's scarred, and the other eye was in danger too, for a while, but it's not now. It's difficult for us to meet, with the Robertsons not wanting me on their land. And Jamie would never step on ours again. When he saw me he said my dad was a fucking maniac, and he looked at me as if something of my dad might be lodged deep inside me, too, where I couldn't see it.

I've gone away. I didn't want the school bus, or the sixth form, or any of it any more. I've got a job in town, working in Argos. I get my room and meals for fifty pounds a week. I go home at weekends, once a month. I've made friends with the girls I never really knew before, who used to sit at the back of the bus. They take me out clubbing with them, and Isobel Farmer's got me a fake ID. Her mum babysits for her on Saturday nights.

Jamie's still there, at home. My mother met Jessie Robertson on the track one day, and she said that Jamie likes the sound of the river. He'll sit by the window all day and listen to it, when he's not feeling so good. The river that's theirs on both sides, the clear and rolling water.

He'll go away some time, but not yet. It takes a while, you know, to get over a thing like that.

Living Out

When you live alone, Ulli thought, you make up a story of your life for yourself. Otherwise, there's nothing. You go out, you come in, you put your bag of shopping on the table. You can't call out, "Guess how much these cost!" or, "You'll never believe what that idiot Henrik did today."

The room is arranged just as you left it. The oranges in the bowl are perhaps a little more wizened. A heap of petals has flopped on to the rug. Those hothouse roses that never last. You don't like them, but you are sorry all the same.

It was the worst part of winter, when everything left over from Christmas just looked tawdry, and there were months of dark lying in wait. Ulli leaned out of her window with the heat of the stove still wreathing her face. The cold made her breath squeak. All day the sky had scarcely lightened, but now there was a dusky smear of red behind the leather-workers' shop. She picked at a crust of ice on her window-sill, and looked down the lane through the bare trees. Two gypsy women in long layered petticoats, red overskirts and laced boots were strolling down the middle of the lane, their voices skirling as if the width of the village lay between them. Both had baskets over their arms. All down the lane shutters creaked open and faces came to the windows as the gypsies passed. Small, watchful village eyes tracked their progress. Ulli's neighbours longed to whip away the bright cloths flung over the baskets. They knew what was under them. Their minds gnawed on a treasure-trove of purloined goods from the village shop, wedding rings left unattended by sinks, and clothes stolen from washing-lines.

The gypsy women made their way lightly down to the crossroads, their heads poised, held high. Their piled black hair was wound up in shawls of fine white wool, printed with roses. They wore jackets of padded citrus-green satin, close-fitting, and below their waists layers of coloured petticoat sprang out and swayed as they moved. Then their crimson overskirts flared as they swerved off into the dusk. Ulli shivered, and swung her double window shut. She was going out. It was too sad to stay in the house while it went dark.

She kneeled in front of her stove and packed in more logs, then pushed in the damper. She was ready to go.

But in the yard her clothes hung on the line in sheaths of ice. The sleeves of her dark-blue sweater spread out stiffly, in blessing. The hem of her quilted skirt was ripped. White shreds of quilting trailed out like frost vapour. Perhaps a dog had got at it.

All day there'd been a row coming from the broken-down hut at the side of the house where she lodged. From time to time men lurched out and braced themselves against the door-frame, blinking. They only used this hut on Saturdays, for illegal drinking-parties. Later on there'd be singing, and a wave of accordion music each time the door opened. Later still, steam would rise as the men staggered out one by one to piss on the frozen soil. They were squat in their padded jackets and their caps with the ear-flaps fastened down. When they had finished pissing they stamped their feet and went back into the hut.

The hut door was tightly closed. The cracked window was full of lamplight and shadows, which moved over Ulli as she went down the path to the main road.

Cars whipped down the dual carriageway out of the city. There was no footpath along it. You had to cross the railway track, which had been laid on the edge of the old village, and still marked a boundary between the village and the city. The railway bridge was outlined by the orange glow of street lights. To Ulli's left a desert of track and points spread away, creaking in the cold. She stepped on to the bridge and it zinged under her weight. She stopped. There was no one else about. She leaned over the bridge parapet and looked out at the straggling poor side of the city, towards the soft tree-furred loops of the horizon. Why hadn't it snowed yet? Perhaps it was too cold. Numb spikes of bushes stuck out of the frozen earth. They needed to be swathed in snow if they were to live through the winter.

Ulli took off one glove and put a finger on the iron bridge-rail. The skin stuck and tore as she pulled her finger away. Away down the track, about four hundred metres from the bridge, she saw the soft bud of a fire. The homeless men were there. They lived out, losing a finger one winter, a couple of toes another. Sometimes a whole life. They sat around their fire, their feet so close to the flames that the rags wrapped round their boots began to smoulder. If they fell asleep they might not feel themselves burning. They called on Satan and a thousand devils, as alcohol flooded them. The drink flushed their faces purple where a mat of capillaries opened to the bite of the frost. Their noses were swollen and chipped, like the turnips which the market-women slashed with their wicked little knives when frost had got into the clumps. Frost would rot human flesh, as it rotted the flesh of the turnips.

They'd be all right if they stayed conscious enough to keep the fire burning on the frost all night. If it was twenty or thirty degrees below, they'd stagger into town, shouldering between them those who could no longer walk. The air would rush past them and the stars and the pavement would swing like boats at a fair as they stumbled. Now they were lords of it all, the seven brothers coming into town, straddling the pavements, bottles clenched in fists: "Saatana! Saatana! The devil take the lot of you!"

But the people hurrying home after the theatre would thrust past them as if they were ghosts.

Would the men make it to the Sports Hall heating grates tonight, Ulli wondered. It was going to be very cold. She'd often seen them sprawling out on the grates, thawing on the heat that had been manufactured for the leisure of other people, for fit, refreshed people who hustled past into their waiting, warm cars.

She watched the men's fire rise, and thought she saw their shadows. But she wasn't afraid of them. None of those men had ever hurt her. Sometimes they blocked her way on the bridge when she walked back late at night. They swayed and called to her, lunging out of the hollows under the bridge steps, but she swore back in their own words, and then they made way for her. The drink slowed them. They moved like spacemen getting used to the gravity of another world.

Now a ribbony darkness fell through the air, brushing her shoulders and her cheeks and the fringes of her shawl. Buildings vanished. She blinked to clear her eyes, and a smudge of darkness blotted out Centrum's top storeys. Night was gathering in thick flakes, a night of black, burning frost. It was too cold to stand still.

She walked briskly through the city centre, edging the stream of people leaving the supermarkets with their Saturday afternoon shopping. They had bought everything. Shampoo suitable for all hair types, full-cream milk, mid-cream milk, low-cream milk, cheese with holes in it and cheese without holes, filter coffee, matting for kitchen floors, Marimekko cloth, sliced sausage and salami marbled with fat, and the last few berries of autumn, straight from the forest and measured with a steel measure from a shiny pail. Celeriac with ice-bruises on it. Light-weight thermal gloves for the kids to wear at their first ice-hockey matches.

The flower-stalls were packing up. The women who kept them had blown out their candle-lanterns and taken the last few unsold flowers from their heated glass cases.

They were wrapping them up quickly in sheets of insulating foam so that they would not wither in the frost. A woman in an expensive racoon coat, their last customer of the day, turned away from a stall carrying a transparent plastic tube. In it there were two velvet-red roses. The woman stared down at the flowers, and her body heat dissolved a spice of perfume into the air as she passed.

Ulli turned off into a side street, then down to the old towpath by the river, crowded in summer, deserted now. She hurried between one lamp and the next, hearing the beat of her boot heels on the frozen soil. They had not yet laid planking across the ice. The current in the middle of the river was still swift and hungry. In another week boardwalks would be laid over the ice for people to cross between the bridges. Down-river, the *Baltic Swan* melted into the darkness as she glanced round for it. It was weeks since she'd last walked down there and heard the wind pulling at its tied sails. Now the masts were bare.

She went on, feeling the warmth and lightness of her steps, the warmth and lightness of her breath. Now the streets seemed to be springing forward to meet her. Light quivered in a halo of freezing particles around the lamps. There, behind a tree, there came an old man fumbling with the front of his clothes. He heard her footsteps and slipped forward, looking for the hole in the darkness out of which her quick female body would come. She didn't look at him. She went by faster than anyone could catch her, into the warm pool of the library entrance which was spilling out students and fat big-eyed children.

She could stop here for a bit. She was bound to meet someone she knew. Nearby, upstairs, there was a café where she could leave her thick coat and shawl with the doorman, and take the evening newspaper off its pole to read while she drank filter coffee and ate a plump cake scented with cardamom.

Already the wind was starting up like the breath of a horse. What was she waiting for? She plunged on down the towpath, where there was nobody walking, past benches which held up their arms to a sun which would not come back for months.

Down here, under the bridge, the current was plucking at the ice. This was where she'd fallen in once, with a group of friends on their way back to somebody's flat after an evening at the students' club. They'd walked out on the ice, each one gripping the hand of the next, crossing the river, drunk. But it was too early in the winter, and the ice had given way with no warning, as if it had never been there. Water went over her, silencing her. Then there was a jumble of ice and cries and arms tearing at her shoulders, scrabbling her back and up and on to the bank. No one was hurt, no one was lost. They'd raced along the street, too breathless with laughter to cry out as the cold speared through their clothes. Later they'd peeled themselves naked to look at their ice-bruises. They had won again. They were invulnerable.

She'd known all the time where she was heading. The little domestic entrance of the church was rimmed with light like a tired eye.

She stamped her feet clean in the warm porch, but the coir matting swamped up the sound. The smell of candles and overcoats and used-up incense made her heart sink. She saw two men slump across a back pew, two women kneeling. Her eyes swam at a glossy precipice of candles in front of the Sacred Heart. She added her own candle, nicking it in among the glitter, and dropped a coin in the candle-box.

She thought of a man she knew, ten years older than her. His blue eyes were slivered with gaps where light jumped like fish. By eleven each night he was crazed over with drink. But he was always gentle with her. He'd go off and do things, and she'd hear bits of the story coming back for weeks. She could have had the whole story if she'd wanted it, but she'd rather not.

He was wanted by the police. He might have got off with a fine, or probation, but now he would go to prison. People said, "It will only be six to nine months, with remission," but she knew better than they did what he was able to bear, even though she had never heard the whole story.

Sometimes, just before he passed out, he would talk to her about this crime. She winced for him as she saw that it had really been nothing. It was as minor as a punctuation mark in the wrong place, but the mark had turned itself into a hook and it had got him. They would drive him to madness. She felt his hand shake in hers.

One Sunday he had gone to the Lutheran cathedral when the service was in progress. He had stood at the back, dressed in light clothes which were wrong for the season. As the service went on he had shadowed over as if the preacher were blowing black clouds over his sun. Of course, she hadn't been there. She could only guess. Had any of them been there? None of his friends who sat in cafés drinking and smoking and telling the story would have been there in that Lutheran cathedral among the clear-faced children turning up their smiles for the preacher. So how had the story got back? He had never told it.

What he had done to begin with was to tear away his clothes from his body. He had nothing to say. None of his cries arrowed across the cathedral as they had arrowed across the thick air of many restaurants. He just took off his clothes. She had never picked up the other bits of this story which would include the hustling and manhandling of his flesh. They said he had committed an assault. Sidesmen and preacher and congregation had wrestled him to the ground. They had even wrapped something round him, for decency. A curtain.

But why had she let him sleep in her bed? She was still asking herself this question. When he turned up outside her door, not seeming to have any other home, she had just let him in. He had taken up the whole bed as he flailed in his dreams. She had wrapped herself up in a quilt by the stove, and scarcely slept. In the morning he'd wanted a drink and she'd had nothing but a quarter-bottle of brandy, so he'd drunk some of that out of a juice-glass and at once he'd come alight, making her cornmeal porridge and talking to her about his mother who had lived and died in the same Karelian village without ever visiting the city which had swallowed up her only son.

His long legs had scissored across her room as he explored her cupboards. He put a lump of butter in the porridge, and he jarred her vase of tulips as he set the porridge on the table. Pollen had showered into the dish.

A stout, poor-looking woman bent awkwardly to take a candle out of the box under the stand. Her fingers were swollen and she fumbled as she lit her candle from Ulli's and fitted it into its spiky holder. She wore fingerless gloves like a market woman's. Ulli was sure that she had seen her before, shovelling small herring in the market, shaking them flat across the top of the measure. The woman clambered to her knees and stripped off her gloves to pray.

The priest came out of the confessional and wiped his hand across his forehead as he turned to straighten a pile of missals. He had sweat on his face. She smiled to think that he had his own private stove in there, his sauna for sin. But she liked him, with his bit of a smile for everyone, and his greenish-black trousers which he probably thought were a bargain. He knew he wasn't important here in this Lutheran city, with his cargo of immigrants and strangers and poor people, and his little cave of a church. Ulli looked into the burning candles, away from him. She did not want him to come across to her, to ask her how her studies were going and had she the time to do a little job for him . . .

Ulli bowed her head and spread her fingers so that she looked through bars of candle-glitter and darkness. The priest was scraping wax off the back of a missal with his thumbnail, not looking round, his back still and alert. Five people in the church with silence between them.

They are in the bar together.

"It's noisy in here. Isn't it too noisy for you in here, Ulli?" he asks, on a rising note of panic.

She picks up her bag and says, "Yes, it's too noisy in here. I can't stand it either. Let's go."

Then he laughs and throws his head back so that light really does blaze in his blue flawed eyes and he says with the passion and anger and challenge of someone who's been waiting years to be proved right, "It's too noisy for her too! Ulli, you can hear it, can't you? You can hear it?"

And she's as weak as ever. She holds on to his dry and burning hand and says, "Yes, let's go, let's find somewhere quieter."

It's not until they are out in the bare, freezing, still street again that he stands rigid and shakes his head violently in horror and fear, knowing now that he will never clear the noises out of it. Then an aeroplane passes overhead so high she can scarcely hear it, but he cries out as it scrapes against the tender membrane of his inner ear and he drops her hand and goes off down the street, lurching slightly as if he can't keep his balance, but still going faster than she can follow, running. She cannot catch him.

I will stop thinking of it, Ulli said to herself. *I will make mysef not think about it any more.* She took her hands away from her face. Her fingers were white where her blood had drained from them. She flexed them, watched the knuckles stretch against her skin. She watched her muscles going about their work, perfectly.

The market woman shivered and finished her prayer. She hoisted herself up from her knees and flickered the sign of the cross over her body. Her candle dipped then burned straight, taller than Ulli's.

When you live alone, you have to make up a story. Otherwise, there's nothing. I went out, I came in. He ran away up the street faster than I could follow. He is in prison now.

Mason's Mini-break

"They've used that awful photo of you again," remarked Cat from the window-sill. She had half the supplements and I had the other half. We weren't buying every single paper any more, the way we had for weeks, but we were heavy newspaper readers anyway. Especially on wet winter weekends after breakfast in small West Yorkshire hotels where we didn't know anyone.

"What? Let me have a look. What are they playing at — I *told* them not to use that one —"

"Wait a minute, I'm still reading the article."

"What's it say? Is it good?"

"It's not about you. It's just on the same page," mumbled Cat dismissively. I stared over her shoulder. The photo had been taken as Cat and I stumbled home at two a.m. the night of the award ceremony. I looked drunk, shifty and twenty pounds overweight. There was no trace of how I'd really been that night, with champagne singing in my blood. *I'd done it*. I'd done it, and no one was ever going to be able to take that away. My mouth was open in the photograph, and I was smiling stupidly.

I looked past Cat's elbow down the wet cobbled village street. It sloped away sharply, lined with black, secret-looking little houses. I knew I'd never get Cat out walking in weather like this. Cat's a mathematician, and she's always got her laptop with her, the way some women have their handbags.

I'd bought all the right stuff. Boots, waxed cotton jacket, thick socks, waterproof map. The cool moist air felt good against my face after the stuffy hotel. Judy, the receptionist, had told me there was a track which turned off the village street and led down to the river in the valley. "It's very quiet, you won't meet anyone there. I expect you're looking for ideas, aren't you? For the next one." I nodded. No point trying to explain how these things work.

It was still raining and the valley was full of fine white mist. The moor-top and the hills had been hidden since we'd arrived. Cat said perhaps they weren't there at all. Really there was a motorway service station just outside the village — couldn't I hear the hum? "Wind farms," I said, a bit crossly. When you're paying quite a lot of money to be miles from traffic, it's annoying to find out how industrial the wind can sound.

It felt better once I'd got going. The rain ran off my boots and jacket just as it was supposed to. I turned up my collar, pulled down my cap and wished I had a stick. This country business wasn't as complicated as people tried to make out.

The track got steeper and rougher. The backs of my legs began to hurt, then I slipped on a patch of raw mud and only saved myself by grabbing at the bank, and the next thing there was blood on my jacket. I sucked the scratches and swore. Still, I wanted to get down to the river even more now, for some reason. I couldn't imagine why they'd built a track like this all the way down here. It was paved with heavy stones, like huge cobbles. You could have run a juggernaut over them. They were worn away, and slippery. Then the track bent sharply, and there was the river, full and yellow and noisy. There was a bridge over it, made from dark stone like the village houses.

At the other side of the bridge there was a low flat stone wedged into the parapet, like a jump seat in a taxi. A girl had settled in it, fitting quietly into the angle of the stone as if she'd been there for a long time. She was leaning forward, writing.

I came towards her slowly. She hadn't heard me through the noise of the river. No, she wasn't writing. She was sketching the trees on a little block of paper. Now I was closer I could see she wasn't a girl. She was older than Cat.

I like watching people do things. Her pencil made very tiny, precise little strokes on the paper. Judy'd mentioned that there were lots of ageing hippies around, who'd bought cottages on the moors when they were dirt-cheap. They did bed-and-breakfast, Tarot readings, rebirthing, aromatherapy. This woman must be one of them, to judge from her clothes. An alternative person. However, it was hard to imagine the quiet figure in front of me grunting her way through a rebirthing session.

Suddenly she looked up. She nodded, but she didn't speak. Then she bent over her work again, shutting me out. I was close enough to see that the drawing wasn't bad, in a painstaking way. She was shading in soft shadows with her pencil. I was curious. I wanted to talk to her, partly because she so obviously didn't want to talk to me.

"Can you tell me where the track goes after it crosses the bridge?" I asked.

"It goes nowhere," she replied quietly.

The river was loud, and I wasn't sure I'd heard right, so I went on, "I'm only here for a couple of days, you see. I don't know the area."

"You're a visitor, then?"

I could tell she was local from her voice. She had a thick accent, much thicker than Judy's. But I'm good with accents. It's to do with being a writer, I suppose. Her eyes were too big for her face. That's not to say she was pretty. I'd thought she was shy at first, but she wasn't. She was just more interested in what she was doing than she was in me. For some reason, I wanted to change that.

"Yes, we live in London. I'm a writer."

Her pencil stopped moving. Then she said, "A writer. Do you live by your work?"

I smiled. It's what everyone always wants to know. You're a writer? How interesting. Have you had anything published? Do you actually earn money from it, real money, the kind that goes into the bank and pays the gas bill and the mortgage? And now at last I didn't have to do all the explaining any more, about Cat's work and me lecturing part-time and writing two days a week. I could just tell her my name. Most people who knew anything about writing would have heard of it, and the ones who hadn't didn't matter anyway.

"I write novels," I said. "You might have heard of my new one, *Dark World* — it came out a few months ago."

She looked unsure.

"It got the Booker," I said. I'm getting used to saying that now. The Booker. A bit throwaway, but not too throwaway. "Of course these things are a bit of a lottery. But useful. Not that anyone actually reads all the hype. I'm Richard Mason, though most people call me Dick." And I smiled, in the way I'd smiled for the *Observer* photographer. Cat had framed that article. The light was marvellous: stormy background, my features brilliantly distinct. And thin. I wondered if this woman had seen it. She murmured something which might have been her name, but again I didn't catch it. Too much river.

"I like your drawing," I said. "Do you sell your work?" It was flattery, but not too gross. Her sketch might have sold, in a local tea-shop.

"No," she said, "I draw for pleasure. But I write, too."

"Do you?" I asked, carefully emptying my voice of expression. Sometimes that does the trick.

"Yes. I've published a volume of verse. Not under my own name, of course."

Oh, Jesus Christ on a bicycle. A volume of verse. I could see it as clearly as if she'd got it there on her lap: the awful title, the duff cover. Published by one of those vanity presses that advertise in the back of the Sunday papers. And she'd have chosen a pen-name for herself, thinking that was what authors did. The pen-name would be prettier than her own.

"And I have completed a novel," she went on, "although it has not yet found a publisher."

Her hands were folded neatly in her lap, and her face was pale against the dark stone of the bridge. She really was tiny; half the size of Cat. I could just see her printing out the wretched novel for the twentieth time on her Amstrad, sending it off to the next publisher on the list she'd got from the *Writers' and Artists' Yearbook*. You could tell by looking at her that she wouldn't give up easily.

"I'm thinking of starting another novel. I have an idea in mind," she went on.

"That's great," I said quickly, following rule two: *Never ask what the novel's about.* Then I smiled encouragingly. "Don't let the — don't let them grind you down." For some reason I simply couldn't say the word "bastards" to her.

Her lips curled in a small secret smile. *"Ah'm thinking of starting anuther novel."* I'll bet you are, I thought. A nice long novel all about rain and rebirthing. She picked up her pencil again and said, "You will find there is a path along the river, Mr Mason."

I was dismissed, but now I didn't want to go. "Do you live up in the village?" I asked.

"I live some miles away, but I am visiting friends here," she conceded, looking as if she felt I asked too many questions. Her drawing wasn't that great, but she knew all about the put-down. Her pencil darkened the shadow of a beech tree.

I was beginning to feel a fool standing there. "Goodbye, then. Good luck with the drawing — and that book!" I said, and turned to stride off up the track to the village. But I slipped almost at once and went down on one knee, banging it hard on the stone. I heard her say, "Are you hurt, Mr Mason?" but I pretended not to hear. It had all got rather embarrassing.

"Goodbye, Mr Mason. Be careful," she called softly. I didn't look back. I knew just how she'd be smiling.

Cat wasn't at the hotel when I got back, and nor was the car. I had a hot bath, then lunch and a chat with Judy, then I waited. Cat didn't come back until half past four, when I was in the lounge having tea.

"Oh Dick, I've had a great time! I've been over to Haworth. And there was hardly anybody there because of the fog on the moors, so I had the Parsonage to myself. It's wonderful — you can't imagine."

"It must have been. You've been away six hours."

"Was it as long as that? It didn't seem like it. I thought you'd be out walking for ages. I've bought some postcards, look, and a biography of Charlotte Brontë. She had the most extraordinary life, not at all what you'd think. I'm going to read all her books."

"Mmm, yes, it's fascinating stuff," I said. Standard rhubarb for a writer I ought to have read but actually haven't. Somehow the thought of those Brontës has always got me down.

Cat dropped the book and postcards on the table. There was a portrait of a woman on the book cover.

"Jesus," I said.

"I know it's not brilliant, but her brother did it. He was going to be a painter, but apparently the girls were better at that, too. It's supposed to be very like her, though. I was talking to one of the curators in the museum. I saw a pair of Charlotte's boots — she had the smallest feet you've ever seen."

I stared at Cat, then down at the picture. "Do you think Charlotte Brontë had a Yorkshire accent?" I asked.

Cat looked surprised. "Yes, she did. It said so in one of the books. There were lots of things written by people who knew her. Mind you, they were horrible about her, some of them. Especially in London literary circles," added Cat, looking at me slyly. "Thackeray had the cheek to say she hadn't got a pennyworth of good looks and just wanted to get a man. Amazing how people don't see what's under their noses, isn't it?"

"Yes," I said.

"And I bought you a copy of *Jane Eyre*. I looked at it over lunch in the pub. I've only skimmed so far — but did you know there's a character with the same name as you?"

"What?" I said.

"Dick, whatever's the matter? Has something happened? You look awful."

"No. I'm fine. Tell me," I forced out, "about this character."

"Oh, he's only a minor one. The mad wife's brother. Not a very flattering namesake, I'm afraid, darling. Never mind."

I pasted a grin on my face. It felt very like the way I'd looked in that awful photograph. Bitch. Charlotte, I'll get you for this. *Use everything*, I tell my creative-writing students. *Bad writers borrow, good writers steal.* No need to tell Charlotte that. I heard my own voice echoing back to where she sat. Was I ever going to stop hearing it?

"Good luck with the drawing — and that book!"

Salmon

He skips stones across the quiet grey of the loch. He's good at it, skimming them one at a time down a lane of his own devising, into deep water. Everyone keeps telling him how deep it is, and how cold, as if he'd be stupid enough to swim out alone and drown.

But they aren't here now. They're up on the round heathery hills with their backpacks, tramping for miles. This is where the four of them first met twenty years ago, two girls, two boys, hill-walking. He's seen the pictures they took with their crap camera, even though his mother hid them away. There she was, smiling up at the camera, her face fatter than it is now. His mother in the heather, with her top off. He flushes, and scoops himself far away, into his own life. Her breasts. He flings out a stone which snags on the water and goes down.

This is a sea loch. Seals come in on the tide, their dark heads bobbing. He watches now, squinting into the grey which is dazzling if you look too long. This stone-flipping is not what his fingers want to be doing. They want to be holding a rod, waiting. Waiting for the music of the water to change. Waiting for the tiny thrum, then the tug.

He knows there are salmon here. The best rivers in Scotland, and he can't touch them. He stares out over the loch, all of it so open, every inch of it owned. He knows if he went up-river, sat on those banks, put a rod into that water, someone'd stop him.

He bends down. He selects a stone, a fine flat one, almost warm in his hand, and grainy. He stands, angles his arm, lets the stone fly. One, two, three, four, five . . .

"Seven," says a voice behind him, "that's lucky."

The girl, the daughter of the woman who owns the cottage where they're staying. She is thirteen, maybe fourteen. Yesterday his mother said the girl had skin like a speckled egg. "You know, one of those farm eggs. Exactly like a warm brown speckled egg." Then she glanced at him, and said, "What's the matter, Paul?"

"Why have you always got to talk about people like that? This isn't a theme park."

His mother is stung, as he knew she would be. She hates theme parks, wouldn't dream of going to one.

The girl has thin brown wrists. She picks up a stone, flicks her hand back, lets it go free. The stone flies over the loch, barely touching it. It kisses the water. Six, seven, eight.

"Eight. That's good," he says. His voice comes out croaky, because it's a long time since he's spoken.

She sits down and hugs her arms around her knees as she narrows her eyes to the water. She stares at the buoys which bob where the caged salmon swim, growing fatty and ready for market.

"Do you fish?" he asks her.

She glances round at his face which looks older than she knows he is. "No," she says, "there's no fishing here. Only sea-fishing. It's all private."

"Is it?"

"Up the river it is. You must have seen the notices. There're enough of them."

"I've seen them," he says. Then he picks up another stone, and skims it without looking at her, and speaks to the air and the loch. "I wanted to see salmon. I thought I'd see salmon, coming here."

"You'll see plenty if you go across the loch," she answers, nodding towards the buoys.

"That's not salmon."

He feels the kick of the word. The great silver thing spurting up-river.

"What is it then?"

"They're like battery chickens. Is that all you've got?"

"You don't know anything," she says, "not anything." But that night she drifts past their cottage door. Her mother has drummed it into her not to go there. "While they pay for it, it's theirs. Keep away and leave them in peace." But she's not a little girl now. She drifts by and he drifts after her, following her peat-coloured hair until it melts into the shadow of the rowans. The nights are long and bright. They go upstream snapping the juicy undergrowth, tangling in bracken. She sits still in a cloud of midges and lets them play on her arms and halo her head. Her eyes are sharp on him.

"Wait," she says.

They wait. The river runs fast, sucking the stones. They watch the water. It is quick and brown, like the pelt of an animal.

"There," she says. "There!"

The salmon skims the fast water. Its body is one silver muscle, thrashing upstream. He thinks it looks at him once, then drives on.

"I saw it," he says.

The long evening has jumped into night. They hear the churn of an engine.

"Quick," she says, "they're coming."

"We're not doing anything," he says, but he slides back with her, deep under the trees. It's a four-wheel drive, patrolling the river for poachers.

"We're not doing anything," he thinks, but he says nothing. They are close in the rank summer green, so close he can hardly see her. She is warm. He thinks of her skin, brown and warm, speckled like an egg. The salmon has gone, and the headlights grind away on the opposite shore, into the distance. They hold their breath and stay still longer than they need to, but he does not dare to touch her.

The next day is the last. The cottage let finishes at ten, and then Janet and her mother will clean the place for the next people. Paul is packed into the car, wedged by walking boots and his mother's easel. The other two have gone on already.

As the engine starts he sees Janet at the window. She is not looking at him. As the car begins to move she moves too. She walks a step or two, and then she runs. She runs faster, against the current of speed set up by the car. For a few seconds she keeps up with it. Her freckles and her peat-coloured hair shine at him through the window. Then she falls back, as if she has suddenly realized that she is too old for this.

The Icon Room

"Excuse me! Excuse me!"

Ulli opens her eyes. It's the man at the table next to hers. Something's wrong. She has heard of men eating steak so fast that they choke and fall down dead in restaurants. No one helps them because they think that the men are having heart attacks, and although everybody has read those government pamphlets that show you how to kickstart a failing heart, it's another matter to slash open the shirt of a blue-faced fellow-diner and set about beating his chest with the heel of your hand while you lay your lips against his and taste his saliva mixed with wine. No, if the cause is a lump of badly chewed meat, your best choice of action is to put your arms around the diaphragm of the sufferer then squeeze in sharply, and with luck the lump will be dislodged into his mouth. Then it should be easy to hook out the blockage with a bent finger.

The usual reason the meat is not properly chewed is that the diner has been drinking heavily, swilling down roughly hacked mouthfuls of steak until a piece of meat hits the gullet at the wrong angle and sticks, jamming the airway so thoroughly that not even a whimper passes it.

"Excuse me!"

But when people choke, Ulli realizes, they don't talk. His face is waxy-yellow, like a good potato. There are crimson dabs on his cheeks and forehead. But he's neither drunk nor cyanosed by a throatful of steak. Thin strips of black hair cross his scalp and meet up with the vigorous hair growing out of his ears. He leans towards her and knocks over the single white carnation in its glass funnel which decorates his table.

"Do you by any chance speak Russian?" he asks.

"No, I'm sorry," says Ulli. "No," she corrects herself. Why is she apologizing? Why should this man think that she speaks Russian? "No," she repeats, "I don't speak Russian."

"Of course you don't!" he reassures her eagerly. "Why should you? It was just that I couldn't help noticing your book —"

"It's a translation," she says, holding up the book so that she can show him that the Cyrillic script only runs down the left-hand page.

He tilts the cover so that he can read the title. "I know that translation," he says. "It's not the best, but I like it. It has a charm of its own, hasn't it?"

Ulli looks down at the page. "Perhaps it's charming if you speak Russian," she says.

"I've put it badly," says the man. "The charm's in its transparency. You can see the Russian text through it. When you can do that, what does it matter if it's a bit wooden? But perhaps you don't agree?"

"I've only read the first few poems," says Ulli.

"Which ones? Let me see."

As he takes up the book, the back of his hand brushes lightly against Ulli's palm. He reads, mouthing the words to himself.

"And what about you?" he asks. "Do you believe in the miracle of the resurrection?"

Ulli stares at him. She pushes her chair back a little, away from him. She's got this man wrong. She'd better be off before he gets out a bundle of tracts.

He says quickly, "Or perhaps you don't know those lines."

"I don't think I've got to that poem yet," says Ulli. Thank God, they are talking about poems, not religion. She picks up her tea-glass and drinks in relief.

"Resurrection. Miracle. Not believing . . ." murmurs the man, running his finger down the page. The stiff curls of the carnation are becoming sodden. Ulli fishes the flower out of its spilled water, and rubs it against her lips. Resurrection. She feels two stocky white candles crossed like a pair of scissors against her throat. She is a child who gets tonsillitis over and over. Her sickness mars winter after winter. Her grandmother takes her to church on the feast of St Blaise, to be blessed. The candles cross like cake tongs, like kitchen scissors, like instruments for probing wounds. Their dense cold waxiness appals her. But she will never move away. It is like the whiskeriness of her grandfather's kiss. You must accept these things, to show love. The candles are stocky and blunt. They will not hurt anyone. Now she smells the dank flower-water and feels the dullness of petals against her lips. Her tonsillitis went on for years.

"Do you want to borrow the book?" she asks. "I'm not really reading it. You can give it to the doorman when you've finished. I'm often in here."

"I'd rather think that you were reading it yourself," he says.

"The water's dripping on you," says Ulli.

He mops around in his lap with one of the red paper napkins which are not thick enough to do their job. She sees more of the clean, glistening crown of his head as he bends down. Each part of his face reminds her of a different exotic vegetable: sweet potato, okra, Jerusalem artichoke. Ulli never knows what to do with any of them. She leaves them alone in their high-priced transparent wrapping on the produce gondola, and moves on to the cheap lines. She buys a kilo of imported pears, Ida Marie apples from Belgium, and fat grooved celeriac.

In spite of his black hair and his red-and-yellow cheeks, this man is restful to look at. He is like a Russian doll, weighted and stacked with sweet-smelling wood. But his little black eyes have sore red streaks on the sclera. He reads too much, she thinks. He wears a shirt of limp, thick blue cotton, marked around the buttonholes and cuffs. He has crushed his padded jacket into the seat behind him, rather than give it to the doorman. He has no money to spare, thinks Ulli, but that is just before he lifts his hand as the waitress passes his table, and orders an expensive Gewürztraminer to share with her.

"In honour of poetry," he says.

His wine is too spicy for her, but she drinks half a cold yellow glassful then tilts the rest about from rim to rim while he reads poems to her in Russian. Dark, thick sounds swarm round the two tables. She wonders if his voice is at all like the voice of the poet.

Ulli thinks of the candles of St Blaise. How were they held together in the shape of a cross? Were they stuck with melted wax, or tied with tape? She tries to remember, but she can't, even though she can still feel the pressure of the two joined candles against her throat. Grandma used to tie Ulli's hair back so it would not get in the way. The priest leaned down and shadowed her as he said the prayer and made the sign of the cross over her, then Grandma and Ulli stepped aside as the next wave of thickly bundled men and women and children flattened itself before the altar.

The café swarms with poems: poems read aloud in football stadiums, poems written in prisons, poems declaimed at the funerals of poets. But Ulli has never been able to listen to poetry for more than ten minutes. She yawns under the weight of poems.

"I've got to go," she says, "but why don't you keep the book?"

"Don't go," he says, half-rising from the table himself. "I was just going to ask if you were free this afternoon."

His hand catches the glass and it rings against the metal holder of Ulli's tea-glass. It rings dully. The long restless Sunday afternoon stretches before both their imaginations.

Drinking cups of coffee until your heart bangs and you feel dizzy when you stand up. Walking home the quiet way and standing still while a lick of spring sunlight needles your skin. Prickling all afternoon as you wait for the sound of the telephone bell, which doesn't ring and doesn't ring, until at last you give up and put on your dressing-gown. Then there's the noise of other people's visitors, leaving in a cloud of laughter and smoke and sharp bright goodbyes. You swallow crispbread and cheese and a glass of wine, and go to sleep, holding tight to the curve of the bedclothes as if you are falling of the edge of the world.

"I'm more or less free," says Ulli.

They walk down the long street which runs parallel to the river. He lives in a wooden house like her own, but his house is in the old part of the city, near the Lutheran cathedral. They walk side by side, like any other couple out on a Sunday afternoon.

His house is better than her own. Its silvery wood is smooth and tended. It has no village pile of tarpaulined logs against the front porch, no broken-down drinking-huts under the side windows. Everything is orderly and well kept. The hall smells faintly of disinfectant, strongly of baking coffee-bread. The balusters are beautiful, made of old silky pine, knotted and wreathed and sweet to touch.

They go up the wide shallow stairs side by side. He has two rooms on the second floor, he says. The rest of the house is rented by a family with two young children. He's been living there for years, since before the children were born.

"Do you see much of the children?" she asks, imagining him like an uncle to them, babysitting, remembering birthdays, bringing flowers and chocolates to the mother on Friday evenings.

"No," he says. "Their mother doesn't like them playing in the hallways, so I scarcely hear them. You wouldn't know that there were children in the house."

At once she's convinced that the children are his.

The young wife longs for a child. Her husband is impotent; no, sterile. He had mumps when he was thirteen. But his wife loves him. She goes out into the hallway and she entrances the man who rents two rooms. He is swallowed up with love for her, though he only sees the whisk of her heels and the corner of her dark-green skirt as she goes down to take out the rubbish. Then one day she comes into his room and shuts the door behind her. Without saying anything, she takes off her skirt and lies down on his bed. He makes love to her in the clear light of the afternoon, with the sun on his back like someone's eyes. When it is over she gets up and adjusts her clothes, fastening her waistband with particular care as if the breaking of her marriage vows must have weakened the zips and buttons of her skirt. Then she goes out. Six weeks later she is bent over the toilet-bowl, coughing and spitting up phlegm. You can hear her right across the hallway. It is a miracle. And better than that it is a miracle which has to be believed. And it happens twice.

"So you don't see much of the children," Ulli repeats aloud. They stand still on the landing. Ulli rubs her hand over the baluster knobs. "I like your house," she says.

"I'm lucky to live here," he says. "It has a preservation order on it, so the Council gives our landlord a grant towards maintenance. Otherwise I'm sure he'd sell it. And I'm in the same position as the house myself."

"How do you mean?"

"I have a stipendium from the City Council, for my writing."

Ulli does not ask him what kind of writing he does. She is afraid he will say, "Poetry."

He doesn't bring out a key. The door snicks open with the good click of a well-oiled spring-catch. First there is a tiny lobby strewn with boots and quilted winter clothing. It smells of darkness and rush matting. Then he opens the door to his main room. They step into a space as red as the lit inside of a heart.

The walls are dark, somewhere between brick and crimson. They glow even where they are not laced with the gold of icons, with the gold-and-silver tracery of icons, with Christs in triumph and stern Virgins who hold out their babies on their arms like swords to cleave the world. Over and over, the child gazes out unsmilingly past the strong curve of the Virgin's breast. Over and over Christ lifts a forefinger, to silence, to beckon, to rebuke, to chastise. The baby wakes from his first sleep, as unrumpled as a fall of silk. The saints glitter and listen. The mother of God blazes blue in the shadow of her son. The face of the risen Christ is scored with dark vertical lines like strokes of a cane. Behind him there is a landscape of rocks hollowed by caverns which shelter lions and leopards. Ulli turns away from them to a small painting on wood, soft in rose and yellow.

"That one isn't a true icon," says the man. "Do you know anything about them? Have you heard how they worked, these icon painters?"

"No."

"They had to pray and fast for days to prepare themselves. They believed that was the only way they could paint these icons as they should be painted. Look at the colours. Everything has significance. Nothing is accidental. They didn't paint these icons for us to walk past them in an exhibition. They aren't things you should read about in order to appreciate them. You have to live with them, until you don't even see them any more. The less you can describe them, the more you receive what they have to give. Whatever you want to call it."

"What do you want to call it?"

"I've never been able to decide. I'm not a believer, if that's what you mean."

They are silent. The icons burn on the walls. If she stays in here too long, she'll be patterned and marked by them. An icon-tan.

"Do you sleep in here? With the icons?"

"No, I sleep through there." He crosses the room and opens a door. "Look. This is my bedroom."

It is a small narrow room with a small narrow bed covered in a quilt of unbleached cotton. The walls are pale. The room is monochrome, finished without tints. But when you look at it, after the dazzle of the main room, its shadows are luminous. Ulli feasts her eyes on the bare walls. They rest her as the frozen Baltic rests her in winter when she looks out from the crusted edge of the sea to where the ice joins with the white fume of the horizon. Above the bed there is a drawing of three trees. Two are standing, and one has fallen, toppling so that its branches hook over the branches of the standing trees, making a long cross-ply of angles. The drawing is pencil

111

on paper. In the corner of the picture there is a signature in small neat script: *Pentti Salminen.*

"Is that you?" she asks. "Is that your name?"

"I'm sorry," he says. "How stupid of me. And rude. I've been on my own too long. Imagine bringing you all this way without even telling you my name. I wouldn't have blamed you if you hadn't come. You might have been afraid."

"Why should I be afraid of you? You don't look like anyone to be frightened of. Besides, I didn't tell you my name, either. Perhaps *you* ought to take care."

"I know your name. It's in the front of your book. You'd written it there."

"So I had."

"You have nice handwriting."

She smiles. Her hand roves on the bedcover's nubbed cream and ivory. Nothing in this room is as cheap as it seems.

"I'll get you something to drink," he says.

Ulli turns round and looks back through the doorway at the icons. And where in heaven's name did they all come from? She has never seen icons like these outside an institution. Is he one of those icon-smugglers she has read about, who trawl the poorest, least sophisticated areas of Russia, offering electronic goods in exchange for icons wrapped in felt and hidden in attics for decades? Does he smuggle them back through the Baltic states, having long ago perfected a look of boredom at the frontiers? Does he jog-trot across the long grey spaces of the Baltic on the Tallinn-Helsinki boat?

In the far corner there's a small dark-faced Christ in Triumph, rimmed with rubies. Or are they rubies? She only knows rubies when they are waved under her nose by engaged girlfriends, with the word *ruby* as the most important part of their setting.

She only knows thin chips of ruby in gold engagement rings, not these flowerings of stone. The room is a miracle. She is at home. She reaches behind her and pulls the door shut.

Now they are two dark warm-breathing shapes in the white bedroom.

"The walls in here are too light," she says. "They hurt my eyes."

"If you wanted, I could draw the curtains."

"Yes," she says. "Draw them."

Coosing

Jordan picks up her glass. She doesn't like holding fragile, precious things that belong to someone else. Aunt Amy had a locked cabinet of glasses which came out only at Christmas and Thanksgiving. Jordan never broke one, but she had to watch her hands all through the long dinner, in case they did what they privately longed to do.

"These look like family heirlooms," she says.

"No," says Rose, "I got them in an auction. They were two odd ones, so they went cheap."

Jordan thinks of Rose at the auction, raising her hand. Rose's brown, thin hand with the silver ring on its middle finger. She knows Rose will have hesitated, even for two odd glasses. Nothing that beautiful is cheap. Rose's hand goes up. Rose had a life of which she knows nothing. And yet these last few minutes, since Rose smiled at her like that, a door has opened. You can have it, if you want to. If you can pay for it. The auctioneer nods, noting the bid.

Jordan drinks the wine. It's strong, sweet, less flowery than she expects. She drinks again. She'll be reckless too. Like drinking martini after martini in Luke's Bar with Marty. Stone-cold gin, green olives, she and Marty suddenly, ravenously hungry, eating handfuls of peanuts.

"Which is more degenerate," Marty asked, "afternoons getting drunk or afternoons at the movies?" Degenerate was their word that summer. Outside, the daze of summertime in New York, the metallic shimmer on the streets, the smell of dirty air and gasoline.

"What is it?" asks Rose.

"I'm sorry?"

"You're smiling."

"Oh, I'm just thinking—" she can't explain Marty right now, it's all too complicated — "of a friend of mine. We used to go to this bar and get high at three o'clock in the afternoon. One summer when we took chambermaid jobs in New York City, replacing the regular staff on vacation. We started at six-thirty and worked through till noon. Then we went right home and dressed up to go to the bar."

Rose leans forward, pours more wine to the brim of Jordan's glass. It's elderflower, made by Rose. Jordan lifts and swallows, lifts and swallows. She knows this feeling. Drinking to get drunk, hitting the rhythm. Walking sweetly along the edge between doing what you can safely do and doing what comes naturally.

She thinks of what came next, what she never told anyone. They were staying in an apartment which belonged to friends of Aunt Amy's, who'd gone to their summer place on Long Island. She and Marty took a cab back from the bar, their heads swimming, their faces stretched with laughter. They could barely tell the cab-driver where they wanted to go. They saw him watching

115

them in the mirror. Two drunken broads. Maybe all he was thinking of was that they might throw up on his upholstery. Marty had these white gloves on. Back in the apartment they made coffee, bumping into each other in the kitchen. But as soon as Jordan took the first mouthful a swill of gin and vermouth and peanuts rose in her throat and she just made it to the bathroom before she threw up. She brushed her teeth, washed out her mouth with Listerine. Suddenly she felt wonderful. Being drunk like this was as pure as being a saint. She walked out to Marty in a steady straight line. "You OK?"

"Sure."

She sat down by Marty on the sofa covered with a patchwork throw of the kind all Aunt Amy's friends thought was just perfect.

"This is pretty good stuff for throwing up on, too," said Marty.

Marty was eating a cream-cheese-and-olive sandwich. That summer Marty was mad for olives. Everything she ate had an olive in it somewhere. They were eighteen.

Then she was leaning against Marty and Marty was leaning against her. They were laughing. She caught a tiny snapshot of herself from outside, hard as a diamond. Laughing, her head slipping down against Marty's shoulder, down and down, against her breasts. Into her lap. The strange softness of Marty's body after all the men they'd both necked. How easy it was. None of those rules and stages. On the first date he does this. On the second he can do that. Not that Marty kept any of the rules. Jordan sliding down, helpless, into Marty's lap, watching herself. Laughing helplessly. Jordan's dry, Martini-rimmed kiss, the taste of olives, her own empty stomach. The way the floor felt against her cheek, the lumpiness of a hand-woven rug. Marty still wearing those white gloves. Jordan wondering if Marty was going to take them off.

Rose is leaning towards her, pouring more wine. This close, their faces are naked. Rose is not so young. She has a child of ten, and a history that has nothing to do with Jordan. How did they get here?

One of them leans forward, or maybe the other, and they touch. Their lips press together, solid and awkward so their noses rub too. Jordan's lips are firm and dry. Then they stir on Rose's mouth, just a little. Like being pregnant, thinks Rose. Such a small flutter it might be all in your mind.

It's the first time Rose has ever kissed another woman on the mouth. There's no sound and almost no movement, just this pressure. Jordan puts her right hand on Rose's waist. They stand there, stock still, then slowly draw apart. They draw apart as if they've got all the time in the world. "Well," says Jordan. It is a light syllable, almost without breath.

John Hendra kicks off his boots and lets them lie. Marje's been scrubbing the floor again, spreading out those islands of newspaper that catch on his boots and drive him mad.

"Why don't you pick this stuff up when you've finished?"

"Oh! — John."

Why does she jump like that as if she's expecting someone else to walk in? He kicks the newspaper but there's no satisfaction in it. "Get this muck off the floor when I come home."

She kneels and scrabbles the newspaper up. "The floor wasn't quite dry — I thought you were going down to The Feathers," she says. Her hair is in curlers under a chiffon scarf, scraped up from the pale nape of her neck. He leaves her and crosses to the basket where Sally, his spaniel bitch, is suckling her pups. She looks up at him and whines. He kneels too, rubbing the silky fur behind her ears, running his hand down under her chin until she is loose with pleasure while the pups suck on. He smiles. He'll keep one of the pups, get a good price for the other three, give Sal a rest before he breeds from her again. She's done well. Look at those eyes following him. The intelligence in them.

"Good girl, Sal." He gives her the back of his hand and she nuzzles it. Then he gets up, goes to the scullery and uncovers a dish of stewing steak. He chops the meat finely, breaks in her biscuit, then beats up an egg and binds the mixture with it. She likes that.

Marje looks at him as he comes out with Sally's dish in his hand, opens her mouth, thinks better of it. The pups have finished feeding. Two of them are already asleep, the other two squirm drunkenly over one another in the bottom of the basket.

"Come on then, Sal. What's this?"

She eats cleanly, as always, moving her lips delicately as she chews.

118

Behind him, Marje clears her throat. "John. Did you take the right meat for Sally?"

He doesn't answer.

"Hers was in the blue dish. The green was stewing steak for a pie tomorrow."

He gets up, goes back to the scullery, takes out the blue dish, and walks with it right up to Marje. He takes off the cover. The meat is dogs' meat, brownish, dry, the fat on it hard and streaked. He lifts it up and holds it close to Marje's face, so close he sees her nostrils close in disgust. But she does not dare turn away.

"I've a good mind to make you eat it," he says. "It's more fit for you than it is for her." He sees her swallow, the Adam's apple riding in her throat.

"She's feeding four pups," he enunciates slowly. "Look at her."

Marje stares at the bitch. Sally is looped easily around her pups, her beautiful body shining. Her eyes are pools of love and trust as she gazes back at John Hendra.

"Don't you try buying that filth for her again or I'll cook it for your dinner and stand over you till you've swallowed it. You'll buy her rump steak at three-and-six a pound if I say so. Don't try to make a fool of me again."

Marje swallows again. Her curlers bob with the effort of controlling the trembling of her head.

"Do you hear me?"

"Yes, John."

She clutches her quilted dressing-gown tight at the throat with her thin fingers. He reaches out, puts his hand over hers. She gives a yelp.

"It's all right," he says softly. "Who'd want you, eh, Marje?" But his hands are stronger than hers and he is pulling them down. He reaches down, undoes her sash. She gives her little yelp again, and tries to pull back, but he carries on. The dressing-gown falls open. She wears a short blue nylon nightdress under it, a relic from years back. He doesn't like her wasting money on rubbish. Rubbish is clothes and trying to look like what she's not.

The blue nylon nightdress was bought for her honeymoon. Expensive, slippery new stuff, nylon. Teasing stuff. She wore it the first night. It's old and limp now, not washed out because nylon doesn't do that. She shivers. It has one, two, three buttons. He undoes the top one. She feels the back of his hand on her flesh. His hands are too big for the buttons but he gets the next one open too, and the third, his hands moving across her like huge insects. The two flaps of the nightdress fall apart over her thin chest, her narrow white breasts with their heavy blue veins, bluer than the nightdress itself.

He stares at her. She says nothing, she knows better. Only her quick breath scampering in her throat, her top ribs going up and down, up and down. His right hand comes out, middle finger behind thumb. He waits. Suddenly he flicks her nipple hard.

"Buy steak next time," he says. And then, "What you standing there like that for? Think I haven't seen it before? Someone'd be doing you a favour if they put you out of time, you worn-out bitch."

She fumbles to cover herself. There's a small red mark on her used-up breast, that's all. But he hasn't finished yet. He squats by Sally's basket again, stroking her head rhythmically as she drowses. Not looking at Marje he begins to talk.

"Guess what I seen tonight."

She knows better than to guess. She knots her sash.

"Rose," he says. "Rose Sancreed. Dirty bitch."

Marje is still, eyes wide. If she could stop him telling her she would. It's dangerous knowing things. Afterwards, he'll remember that she knows.

"In the lane with the Yank. Jordan Pennance." His voice is thick and rough. He only talks like this when he wants to, he can talk as good as anybody. "Near as buggery fucking like rabbits on the ground."

Marje breathes out. Suddenly he turns. "Did you know she was like that? Was she like that at school? Touching you up in the girls' toilets?"

Mute, Marje shakes her head. She watches his hand moving over Sally, intimate, tender, aware.

"What d'you make of it, Marje?" he asks. His voice is open, easy, almost as if he's talking to Sally.

Marje's voice will not work. It scratches out a little sound in her throat.

"I asked you a question."

Marje coughs. "I don't know."

"Well, I do. Let her wait. She doesn't know I seen 'em. She'll find out."

He sits still, brooding, gently knuckling the jaw of the sleeping bitch. Very quietly, strayingly, his wife begins to move towards the stairs.

"Marje!"

She stops, one hand up at the neck of her dressing-gown again.

"You wouldn't think of coosing to Rose. Cos if you do I'll know."

He grins. She gives a convulsive shake of the head.

"You make sure of it. You go running off to her while I'm working, I'll know where to find you."

Blaise is picking raspberries, though it's nearly dark, so dark that he finds the fruit by touch. He picks into a flat basket, then empties the berries into punnets on a wooden tray. Sixteen punnets to the tray, and he'll take them down to market in the morning, along with bundles of asparagus and early peas. Long time since we've had a year for raspberries like this one. All that early rain and now the sun. The best soft fruit there is, nothing to beat them. Smell the perfume coming up off those. They look black in this light but they're perfect.

He dips in the leaves. He draws the ripe, fragile fruit off their hulls and lays them down lightly. A late blackbird plunges into the spicy branches of the fig. She's had her nest in there for sure. She clatters down in the leaves, then goes silent. He can see flowers in the strawberry bed from here, picking up whatever light's left and shining it back like stars. That bed's like a knot, flowers and fruit all twisted together. Put some more straw down tomorrow in case it rains, though it won't. Should go back now. One more row, then the tray'll be full and maybe some over. But you don't want to stop when it's like this. By the morning they'll have gone over and begun to spoil.

He slips a berry in his mouth and it melts there, spreading sweetness over his tongue with a drop of acid too, just as it should be for sale tomorrow. He's finding raspberries by knowledge now, not by sight at all, and the moths are out, flitting down the garden. A couple of garden tigers there, woken up by the night, the white on their wings showing. And the bats, though he's too old to hear them. Always get a few flying by that wall there, out of the ivy. Half the world's waking itself up now. A day world and a night world. Funny how you forget that the one's as powerful as the other. Or more. Like when they were kids and used to play out late into the night, up in the hayfields after they'd been mowed. The moon would get on them and they'd go mad, half out of their skins leaping and tussling. Wonder if Rose remembers that.

The gate squeaks. Blaise turns, but the dusk is too thick for him to see across the kitchen garden now. Footsteps crunch down the cinder path. Heavy footsteps. Not a child or a woman. "All right?" he calls.

"Thought I'd kind you here."

He knows the voice. John Hendra, and close to him now. A shadowy outline first and then a man, as if he'd just been made out of the night. He reaches into a pocket and pulls out a pipe. Blaise smells the tobacco as he unrolls his pouch, packs the pipe and tamps it down. There's the flare of a match and a face, sucking in air. He could be anyone coming up for a bit of a smoke and a coose. But being John Hendra, he isn't.

"What do you want?"

"Come up to see you. Give you a word of warning maybe."

"You stick to your cow-walloping. 'F I want a word of warning, I'll ask for one."

"Now then. Don't take me up like that." Suck, puff. The scent of burning tobacco wreathes through that of raspberries. That sickly tobacco he smokes.

"Watch where you're treading," says Blaise. "There's a tray of punnets down by your feet."

"It's about the Yank," says John Hendra. "Nice raspberries you got here."

"She's got a name."

"There's names for women like her, yes," agrees John Hendra pleasantly.

"You got anything to say to me, you better say it."

"All right then. *Jordan Pennance* is up to something with Rose Sancreed. I seen 'em together. Now we know why Rose's been so offish when she ought to be glad of anyone that'll have her, with the kid. 'Bout time you did something about it I reckon."

Blaise doesn't think. His hands are still among the leaves. Immediately the words are out in the air they are true. The smell of John Hendra's tobacco is sickening, overpowering both fruit and flowers. So it's true. Now why's Hendra come here? Just to say that or what else?

"What I reckon is," goes on John Hendra smoothly, lazily, "we ought to put a stop to their carry-on. And you being such a friend of Rose's, I come to you first."

"You told Marje?"

"Course not. Marje don't want to hear their muck. Marje's a decent woman."

"She is," says Blaise.

"No, I told no one. Just you. Not that there aren't plenty who'd like to hear it. You can just see their ears pin back. Rose Sancreed rolling round with the Yank after she's been so touch-me-not. Or maybe she hasn't?"

His insinuations wind round Blaise. He feels like a fly being parcelled up by a spider.

"Not that either of 'em are anything to us, of course. All the same summat's got to be done."

Blaise bends, feels for the last punnet and tips the basket in. A wave of rage breaks in him as he pats down the furry tenderness of the berries. He doesn't have to listen to this. John Hendra's standing too close to him. Watching him like a guard, telling him what to do. Blaise picks up the heavy wooden tray and raises it high in the air. Even in the near-dark John Hendra has a second to sense what is coming. His arm comes up but at that instant Blaise brings down the tray on his head. John Hendra grunts. Blaise throws himself on top of the other man and they go down into the mess of raspberries. The pipe's gone, knocked out of John Hendra's mouth. He's down in the soft dark soil under the canes, his head wedged where Blaise can't get at it. Raspberries patter over his hands. He grunts and drags, hauling the heavy body out so he can get at the face. John Hendra curls tight, backing up against himself. Blaise grabs whatever comes to hand and smashes it on John Hendra's head, but it's light stuff, rubbish, raspberry punnets. The canes are in the way. There's no space to swing his arm for a punch. John Hendra will not fight back. Suddenly the softness of him is too close. Blaise scrambles away, stands, brings back his boot and kicks John Hendra. He wants to kick him in the stomach but he's rolled sideways so the kick finds his ribs. He grunts, will not cry out.

"You'll get more'n that," pants Blaise, 'f you open your mouth about this again. You keep your tongue off of Rose."

There is harsh breathing and an overwhelming smell of sweetness. John Hendra gets up slowly, clutching his face.

"And don't try anything. Any of your hiding and waiting I'll be ready for you." Blaise trembles with the desire to kill John Hendra. "Get out," he says quietly, and John Hendra goes stumbling up the cinder path to the gate. And then, though he'd told him to go, Blaise half wants to call him back. He wants to hold on to the flood of heat and the way everything else vanished as he pounded John Hendra's head. He's wanted to do that for a long time. He bends down, picks up bits of smashed punnet, wet with fruit. No use keeping 'em. His hands are shaking now. Got to move, do something.

He hasn't even got a bowlful of berries left. Why'd he do it? The sweetness of thudding a boot into Hendra's stomach has ebbed. All that's left is a cold trickle of unease. God help Marje Hendra tonight.

Rose is alone when he comes, sitting with her hands clasped round her knees, stirring the fire so the flames break into embers. There's the back door open behind her, and fading streaks of green in the sky over the sea.

"Fancy you coming now!" says Rose. "Just when I was thinking of you."

"What were you thinking?" He drops to his knees by the fire, glad that she's spoken first.

"What've you done to your face?"

He puts up his hand, rubs his cheek. "What?"

"There's something on it. Not blood is it? And on your shirt."

He looks down, sees the dark patches she's seen. "It's juice. I've been picking raspberries."

"Looks like you've been rolling in 'em."

He laughs. Easy to pass it off, but then he says, "I have."

"What d'you mean?"

"Been giving John Hendra a hiding. He came up where I was working." There is a long silence, or at least, no words spoken. Time with nothing in it but the distant sea working away at the rocks.

"Did he," says Rose at last, in a tone he does not recognize. He looks down so as not to see her face. Next time he sees it she'll be a different woman, the one who's heard what he's going to say, who knows what he knows.

"He come looking for it. Saying a lot of lies about you and Jordan Pennance."

He finds he's looked up at her, though he hadn't meant to. The redness of the fire seems to carve her face.

"I ought to of known," she says. "What can you ever do in this rotten place without someone hiding to catch you." She stands up, turning away from him as if he is the one she blames.

"I didn't know anything. I only shut his mouth for him."

"Think it'll stay shut now? You opened it. You marked him, didn't you? Now when he goes running with his story he's got the proof of it. Why'd you hit him if there was nothing in it? They know you like me, same as he does."

The way she says it silences him. She's known all along all those delicate things he thought he'd kept hidden. She talks of his liking for her as if it's common property, the same as John Hendra trying to get her round the back of a barn when he's had a few.

"I can just see you, the pair of you, rolling round thumping each other like I was a bone you'd got between you. Well, I'm not. I've got nothing to do with either of you. And I don't want you feeling good cos you reckon you've fought John Hendra for me. I could've shut him up myself better'n that."

"But, Rose —"

"And I'll fuck Jordan Pennance if I feel like it. Yes, I know. I can't say that. That's your word, isn't it? That's the man's word. *You like to do her, boy? Nice fuck she'd be*. You think I haven't heard all that? Can't you say anything?"

"I couldn't just leave it, could I? Let him say what he liked?"

"Why not? I've been left long enough. I could be left longer," says Rose. "You tell me how long I been left. Everyone round here knows it, let's see if you do. *Here's Rose Sancreed back with a big belly on her. Nice sort of war work that was. Let's watch how she gets on.* So they left me to get on with it. And that's what I'm doing. I don't want you fighting for me. Don't you think you're going to come squeezing in on me like that."

The shaken moment when it might not have been said. The green's gone out of the sky now. Rose won't look at him. She goes to the sink and wipes two mugs dry, slowly, carefully, then hangs them on the dresser hooks. She moves as if he isn't there. He gathers himself, but all he can see is Rose, naked, swimming out from between another woman's legs as if she'd been born there.

The Kiwi-fruit Arbour

Thank God, Ulli thinks, that Jean-Paul never lets her sit in the back of his car. Isabelle can sit in the back, that's fine, surely she can fold away all that leg somewhere, but their visitor must sit in the front and talk to him. He likes the sound of Ulli's French, which apart from being not bad, not bad at all, has a rough edge to it that reminds him that she comes from the wild forests of the north where they are all pagans and worship the sun. Or so he says. Isabelle laughs. They've all remarked how odd it is that of the two girls, Isabelle makes by far the more convincing Scandinavian with her blonde hair and blue eyes. Ulli has given up explaining about Finno-Ugric language groups and the complete difference between Finnish-speaking Finns and Swedish-speaking Finns and real Swedes. She's beginning to know that for the Colbert family reality subsists only within French, so infinite in its possibilities for jokes, satire, explanation and deep, offhand pride.

Jean-Paul never tires of mapping out landscapes for Ulli, stripping away the present moment of languid sun and ice-cream to explain a disharmony of architecture along the sea-front, and the self-willed millionaire pride which has caused it; to tell her why the hedges run wide as lanes between the apple orchards; to point out the beaches where Albertine once played Diabolo, and the little band of girls once gathered to torment and enchant Marcel Proust.

White dust sprays up from the car ahead. Jean-Paul's windscreen is splodged with dead midges which won't wipe off. The little potholed road runs between huge fields of ripe sunflowers. Here, twenty miles north of the Colberts' summer house, the fields become enormous. There's a reason for this, too, but Ulli hasn't retained it. How can anybody go on and on feeling so sick for so long without ever actually vomiting? It's far worse than the nausea of her childhood, when she used to go to bed with a tight, sick stomach after listening on the stairs to the rows between her parents. There's no pretending any more. Ulli can conjugate the verb *to be pregnant* in her sleep.

I have heen pregnant for six weeks . . . seven weeks . . . eight weeks . . .

I shall be pregnant for nine months

According to the test, I am pregnant

By the time I go home, I shall have been pregnant for fourteen weeks.

She has learned the jussive mood of the verb:

Let me not be pregnant!

And she's becoming familiar with the sweet, escaping conditionals:

If only I weren't pregnant

If I hadn't become pregnant

Just think, what if after all I'm not pregnant?

But it's a private grammar. She hasn't taught it to anybody else. Jorma hasn't yet had to learn the sad past tense of the verb *to make pregnant*:

I have made Ulli pregnant.

For Jorma, only the past tense seems to apply. You can't say,

Jorma is making Ulli pregnant,

or

Jorma will have been making Ulli pregnant.

No, even though Ulli is incontrovertibly pregnant in the present tense, and making herself (or being made) more pregnant with each day that passes, Jorma's role refuses to come out of the past tense.

So maybe in the end it is grammar which has kept Ulli from writing to Jorma to acquaint him with the new language she's had to learn, in her night-study before mirror and toilet, in her constant, daily, casual-seeming search for public lavatories and other secluded places where she can lean her forehead against cool surfaces and try unsuccessfully to rid herself of the acid knot in her stomach.

Grammar and distance. Words on paper. The whole question of how you put things. Ulli has read enough to know that there are conventions covering the way in which women convey such information to men. But she and Jorma just don't seem old enough for those patterns of *taking advantage, getting into trouble* or *doing the right thing.*

And then she thinks of Jorma's parents and she shivers. Just what they knew all along.

A silly girl, a silly little girl. If a pair of children like that were going to do it, couldn't they have had the sense to take precautions? Or perhaps this particular little girl hadn't really wanted to be that careful? Perhaps she'd had something else in mind? Hmmm?

Well, sometimes a bit of plain speaking has to be done. Let us, as Jorma's parents, make one thing quite clear: there can be absolutey no question of Jorma's being in a position to tie himself down, or support a child. At least eight years of study lie ahead of him. These things have got to be looked at sensibly.

As it happens, we do know an awfully nice doctor, very discreet and a first-class reputation. We've only to say you're the daughter of friends of ours who's come to us for help, and that's all he'll need to know. He won't ask any awkward questions.

Never, never, thinks Ulli, will she write the words which will permit such a conversation to take place. But she can trust Jorma, can't she? If she asks him not to tell his parents, he won't, will he?

But Ulli's only sixteen, Jorma darling! How can she possibly know what's best, even for herself? And she's certainly not thinking about what's best for you, I can assure you! The trouble is, Jorma, that with a girl from such a very different background, everything has to be spelled out. She simply doesn't understand. And I suppose she's got hold of the idea that there's plenty of money to spare. People like that have no idea of the kind of commitments we have.

Jesus, Jesus, help me, prays Ulli, in the vocative case.

* * *

133

The sunflowers are a bright, blinding yellow. They lift up their heavy faces towards the afternoon sun. They are ripe, and within a couple of weeks they'll be taken away to be crushed for oil. Ulli supposes that there must be special sunflower mills where thick metal plates fold one over the other to crush the seeds.

"Only four kilometres to go!" shouts Isabelle from the back. The car is extremely noisy, because Jean-Paul keeps the sun-roof down all the time. This is good for nausea, and with the side windows open as well there's a constant buffet of warm air, soothing and drugging.

"Was there a signpost?" asks Jean-Paul.

"I'm reading the map, measuring from the last crossroads."

"OK. Let's stop and have a drink."

They continue along the road as before, then all at once Jean-Paul sees a bare patch of earth and grass by the sunflowers, pulls the wheel over and brakes hard. The car judders, rocks, then stops. They all lie back in the seats for a moment, stunned, smelling hot metal and earth. A bird sings out of a scrubby bush.

Isabelle unwinds her legs. She's been lying along the back seat, with her toes hooked through an attachment to the car roof. Her legs are long, slender and beautifully shaped. From the waist down, she's perfect, like a mermaid in reverse. Then above there's her rubbery, laughing face with its irregular teeth, and eyes which squeeze up into slits against the sun or a good joke. She has big, squashy breasts, and her shoulders are muscled from swimming competitions. Today she's wearing an old, off-white cotton jersey and a pair of shorts which

134

are stained with sun and salt-water. Jean-Paul is correctly dressed for château-visiting in his dark linen trousers and shirt with a tiny soft check of green and tobacco-brown. It's the kind of shirt you want to touch.

"You get the bottle out of the boot," Isabelle orders her brother. "Ulli looks awful, I'm sure she ought to have a drink straight away."

And it's true that the ground underneath Ulli doesn't seem to have stopped moving, even though the car has. She hasn't got the strength to move. A sunflower looms up at the window as a breeze carries it forward on its big rough stem. Even if it slapped her in the eye, she couldn't do anything about it. The middle of the sunflower is full of tiny black insects, clambering over one another and over the sticky seeds. She looks away, up to the sky, but to her alarm the tiny black wriggling insects are up there, too, crawling over one another, getting thicker and thicker.

"Ulli! Ulli! Are you all right? What's the matter?"

"Spread the rug out, Isabelle."

Their voices clang like church bells under water. But just as the sky gets so dark she can't see anything, she feels Jean-Paul's hands at the nape of her neck, forcing her head down. Then there's the prickle of stalks under the rug and she's all right again. Everything's swinging back into shape.

"No, don't move yet. Have a drink."

It's mineral water, not wine, and it's as blessedly tasteless as a mouthful of air. She swallows greedily. Isabelle takes the empty glass from her hands.

"You're freezing!" she exclaims. "You're really ill!"

Ulli opens her eyes and sees Isabelle on her knees in front of her, holding the glass, her skin breathing violent health and life. "No, I'm OK now," she says. "I think it was too hot for me in the car, that was all."

"I'll fetch the wine," says Isabelle, and disappears round the back of the car.

"Don't drink any," says Jean-Paul quietly. "You're really not too good, are you?"

Ulli says nothing. If she speaks, she'll just cry.

For half an hour they don't move. Ulli lies on the rug. Isabelle sits hugging her knees, sipping from her glass of chalky white wine. It's the wine they drink for everyday. They don't drink a lot, any of them, but there's always wine on the table, or chilling in the fridge. No one gets excited about it. Ulli cannot imagine beginning to explain to them the way her father drinks. Isabelle sips slowly, and holds up her glass to look at the sunflowers through the wine. Then she's had enough, and she flicks the dregs of her wine into the dust.

Jean-Paul lies on his stomach, making notes in the battered paperback textbook on thoracic surgery which he's been carrying everywhere this week, stuffed in one of his pockets. He frowns, and scribbles a question-mark in the margin. A small hot breeze gets up and rustles the sunflower stalks. They rub against one another with a dry, brittle sound, lighter than the chirring of the crickets which goes on like a headache all the time. Sometimes a car goes by. They hear it when it's way off, making a faint sound that might be a breath of wind or an aeroplane high up crossing the Channel, then it separates itself from all other sounds and it couldn't be anything but a car, revving over the potholes and jolting its way past them in a haze of dust and exhaust. Then it's gone. The noise is immediately so much part of the past that the car could have gone by hours ago or even days ago.

Jean-Paul's battered gun-metal Citroën grows hot and dangerous in the sunshine. It look like a weapon which will explode as soon as it's touched. An oily shimmer of heat vibrates over the bonnet. Ulli thinks of water and petrol and oil being drawn out of its innards, evaporating into the hot afternoon, leaving the Citroën's carcass as dry as a picked bone.

Jean-Paul gets up and puts the book back in his pocket. He goes over to the car and opens all the doors to cool the interior before they drive on. He walks back to the girls and stands over Ulli so that his face is a blank disc against the intense light.

"Would you prefer to go back, Ulli? We can come to the château another time."

"I'm fine. It would be a pity not to go," says Ulli. She can't face the idea of a long, hot return journey just yet. Later on, surely it will have cooled down? And then perhaps they'll go back another way, on a road which isn't so rough. The château will be cool and green and dark. There'll be a long avenue of plane trees, casting a heavy shade. There'll be a rose garden with white roses glowing against the bronze of the leaves. Inside, battered tapestries on the walls, telling stories of loss and flight. Forests of tapestries, slit windows like mirrors which make the plain, baked landscape look mysterious and shadowy. There'll be a wide staircase with broad, shallow stone steps, grooved by centuries of feet. The chill of the stone will strike up so that Isabelle shivers and rubs one long bare leg against another, and wishes she hadn't worn her shorts.

There'll be a guide who tells his stories slowly enough that Ulli can follow every word. It's the history of the family that she wants to hear. How they rode out of their gateways when the forest still lapped from here to Paris. How they rode in again with their clothes white with dust, how they fell in love and remained faithful to one another through years of war, how they betrayed one another and gave birth in secret, biting on their sheets to silence themselves. Her own family has no history.

They must carry on to the château. Ulli dreads messing up plans, getting in the way, being a drag on Isabelle and Jean-Paul. She's never imagined that a brother and sister would choose to spend their time together in the way Jean-Paul and Isabelle do, and that they'd draw Ulli in so that she felt she'd always been here, part of the plans and the arrangements and the shaping of each new hot day.

Every morning Isabelle gets out map and *Guide Michelin* and notebook and pencil and asks Ulli what she would most like to do, what she would most like to see. They scan the pen-and-ink drawings of châteaux and cathedrals, and read the history of battles. But Ulli is no help because she can scarcely think ahead of her enjoyment of this present moment, drinking coffee outside at the unsteady garden table while Isabelle's mother prepares to go shopping. The cane garden chairs are cold under Ulli's thighs. The sun's already warm on her hands, lighting up the slippery half-moons of fruit buried in the jam in its glass dish. Their morning café au fait goes cold quickly in its shallow bowls. Ulli eats slice after slice of plain bread. There are big red gooseberries on the table too, so ripe they have stretched their skins until you can see the pips bunched close to the surface of the fruit.

Jean-Paul has two weeks' holiday from his internship. He is a medical student, studying surgery in Paris. The first two days he's home, he scarcely speaks. His skin is sallow with fatigue, and his yellow eyes droop even while he's eating. He spends the entire day lying on the old blue steamer chair by the kiwi-fruit arbour. When the shade moves round on to him he staggers up and pushes the chair back into the sun. His mother brings him cloudy lemonade and tells him to go back to sleep. Then she walks away down the path to the house, carrying the tray, her head up as she breathes in the perfumes of the garden.

Ulli watches the movement of her strong, rounded calves in their high-heeled sandals. She thinks Isabelle's mother is beautiful. She doesn't dress at all like the Frenchwoman of Ulli's imagination. She is not small and dark and chic and clever with accessories. She is big-boned, but the wide features which battle in Isabelle's face seem to have made some sudden, last-minute peace in the face of Mme Colbert. She teaches film studies with a special interest in women and film. Ulli has never met anybody like Isabelle's mother, but Isabelle seems to take everything for granted. Of course, one's mother is a feminist; of course, one's mother writes articles in journals and gets invitations to all the film festivals; of course, one's mother wears a scrap of bikini on the beach and doesn't care that there are the stretchmarks of two pregnancies on her stomach; of course, one's mother gives herself a good whack of the glazed pear tart rather than sharing it out between the children and leaving only a sliver for herself . . . *Mais bien sûr, Ulli!* Of course it's OK, Ulli! Go ahead! Help yourself! *Mais pourquoi pas, Ulli?*

* * *

The garden is so beautiful. Perhaps, if Ulli could choose, she would never go out of it. At the top of the garden there are a dozen apple trees in rough grass. The grass is wet with dew long after the rest of the garden is dry. Little hard green apples fall under the trees, too sour even to nibble. Ulli lies on her back and looks up through the branches into the sky, which is streaked with high cirrus cloud and jet vapour-trails, so high she never hears the planes. She wriggles her body until it lies comfortably along the bumps and rises of the earth. The grass has been cut recently, and the mowings are scattered under the trees, drying to hay, sweetened by withering clover. Beyond, there's a rising wall of green turf topped by hawthorns, then the land drops away to the fields which run down to the sea. The sky is white and wide, and the sea looks dark. You can smell it, and on one misty white day Ulli tasted its salt on the grass.

Jean-Paul lies in the sun until his sallowness changes to tan, and he opens his eyes. They are yellow as a cat's. He doesn't look at all like Isabelle. He is like his father, who stays in Paris all week and comes down at weekends smelling of the city. But soon it'll be the *grandes vacances* and the father too will be down here on his holidays.

The man who comes in to mow the rough grass with a big petrol mower tells Ulli the story of the liberation. He was a boy of eight, crouched in a cellar, hearing gunfire. The thing was, nobody knew what was happening. You see, at the time you don't know that this is the liberation and everything's going to be OK in a few weeks. It isn't history yet, you're just stuck in the middle of it. You see terrible explosions and those Boches tearing around the village. Someone once said there's nothing worse than an army in retreat, and now you know it's true. They're taking pot-shots round corners, they don't care who's in the way. Then they've gone, but you don't dare believe they won't be back. There's a pall of smoke so thick you can't see the men coming up out of the sea, but there are streaks of fire in the smoke and then you hear the shells landing near you, as if it's you they're after. And someone in the village goes mad and rings the church bells, but the Boches haven't gone yet and they turn round and fire at the church. You can still see the marks on the bells. We all heard the bells ring.

Ulli takes back his empty glass. He thanks her, formally, and turns away to chop the grass at the top of the bank with a scythe. From the bank he can see the whole line of the coast.

Yes, if she could choose, Ulli would stay in the garden.

* * *

"Are you sure you want to go on, Ulli?" asks Isabelle. "You don't look too good to me, even now. Don't worry about us, we don't care either way."

"I'm OK, really. And I do want to see the château."

The car is as hot as ever, but it's a short drive now, and Ulli doesn't feel too bad. They park outside the château. You're supposed to walk up the drive, after you've paid. The drive is just as long as Ulli's imagined it, but the trees on either side are limes, not planes. They have been strictly pollarded, so there's no luxuriant canopy of green. The edge of the turf at each side of the drive is sliced through in a clean sword-line. The gravel under their feet is white and sparkly and it has the satisfying crunchy texture of gravel which has been spread thickly, with no expense spared.

But there's something happening to Ulli which is beginning to outweigh the trees and the noise of the gravel and the ticket of entry in her hand, which weighs heavier even than the steep grey château which has just appeared at the end of the drive. At first it is an intense irritability in every particle of her flesh, like an electric storm. The worst thing is, she just doesn't know what's happening to her. Ulli has always been able to cope with things better once she's been able to put a name to them. *Domestic violence. Unfaithfulness. Falling in love. Virgin. Non-virgin.*

The way you are, you balance. That's what Jorma said, when he saw her breasts. But that was before the declension of pregnancy.

Ulli stumbles, and Jean-Paul catches hold of her arm. Ulli feels sweat break out over her face, and at the same moment, like the release of the storm which has been trying to earth itself in her, she knows she's going to vomit. She grips Jean-Paul's arm and digs in. They are by a bench and Jean-Paul is sitting her down. The weight lifts off her again and she looks out and away over the small formal paddocks which surround the landscaped grounds of the château. A girl in English riding-clothes is running down the paddock, looking behind her and laughing. Her pale pony-tailed hair bumps up and down against her back. Behind her come a younger girl and a man of about forty. He's handsome and dark, dressed in a dark-green glazed-cotton jacket and jodhpurs, and a flat cap. The little girl has not been riding. She has fair hair so perfectly cut that it looks Japanese, and she's wearing a "simple" cotton frock with smocking across the chest and a long flying sash. The older girl slows and they catch up with her. They walk confidently across the garden, ignoring the tourists and the signs pointing to the entrance. They open the door which says ENTRY FORBIDDEN, then disappear into the château.

"I'm going to be sick," says Ulli, and Isabelle's face distorts itself in a shiver of disgust.

"She can't bear people being sick," says Jean-Paul. "I'll come with you, Ulli."

In the big cool hall of the château there's nobody. One guided tour has just begun. They can hear the voices echoing down the stairs. Jean-Paul raps on the caretaker's door, and when a young man with his thumb in a book comes out he tells him that the young lady is not well, is there a cloakroom? The young man has to open it up with a key. It's not usually open to the public, he explains, there is a public toilet at the gates. Jean-Paul pushes Ulli inside and stands by the door.

"Listen, Ulli, I'm just out here," he says. "If you need me, I'll come in." But she won't call him. This has nothing to do with Isabelle and Jean-Paul. This is Ulli's affair, the affair of people who don't have kiwi arbours or beautiful mothers, who are silly little girls who ought to be got out of the way. This is the affair of people who are "exceptionally gifted", and win scholarships to study in Paris and stay in the French countryside with families who want to offer some of their brimming wealth and principle to those whom they would never otherwise meet.

Jean-Paul takes her weight as they come out into the dark hall. The tour is over and tourists mill about taking pictures of the staircase. The caretaker, who has been hovering with his book, asks Jean-Paul, "Everything all right?"

"We'll take her home," says Jean-Paul. "Pity to miss the tour, but we'll come another time."

As they go down the lime avenue, passing through cage-bars of light and shade, Ulli opens her hands where the unused ticket of entry is damp and crushed.

Does Isabelle's mother know, or does she not know? The days are as hot as ever, beginning with a fresh light dawn which always wakes Ulli, going on to a white midday when she always sleeps. It doesn't take more than two or three days to create an *always* when you're ill in bed. Words roll in Ulli's mind like pebbles turned by waves until they become smooth and easy to handle.

Pregnant. Not pregnant. Mother-to-be. Young girl with all her life in front of her. Everyone says how wonderfully Ulli's French is coming on.

Jean-Paul comes in to play cards in the evenings, with Isabelle. His yellow eyes glitter as he wins time after time. Ulli likes Isabelle and Jean-Paul to be there, though they tire her. She can feel even the slight weight of the cards through her bedclothes. The bedroom smells of peaches, but Ulli has no appetite.

Only another two weeks, thinks Ulli. Then I can go home. She'll go home, to the bathroom with its tangle of socks without partners and laddered tights. Jorma will be back from camp soon. He'd be the same Jorma, to whom none of this has happened. Will he be able to learn the new grammar she's had to learn? Will she be able to teach him to conjugate the verb *to be pregnant*?

Jorma is useless at languages. He'll run, she knows. He'll run away, pretending he doesn't understand, into the big wooden bedroom at the top of his parents' architect-designed house.

"Are you getting tired, my little friend?" asks Jean-Paul. "Do you want us to go?"

"No, I'm fine. I was just thinking of home."

"Were you homesick?"

"I don't think so. No."

"You know, Maman, years ago, she signed the declaration that women signed, saying they had had abortions. You know the one. Lots of film stars signed it," says Isabelle.

There's silence in the room. Ulli's body is like a drum, echoing to Isabelle's words. She feels purified, and far away from herself. The grammar of pregnancy recedes and recedes. It is faint now, so faint she can hardly hear it.

Mon enfant, ma soeur,
songe à la douceur . . .

There's a smell of baking bread in the house. How can that be?

"It's Maman," says Isabelle. "She's making some kind of special bread they have in Vienna. You can't get it here."

"Vienna," says Ulli. "Why Vienna?"

"She was there when she was young. She went there when she was eighteen, to learn German. But really I think Grandmère wanted her out of the way. Maman was seeing too much of somebody she didn't like."

Isabelle's eye go into slits. Perhaps she's smiling, perhaps not. Jean-Paul waits with the slick cards in his hand, ready to deal.

"And did she stop seeing him?" asks Ulli.

"Yes, in the end I think it just died. There were so many new people in Vienna, and she was away from home. She realized that was what she'd wanted all the time. New people. Then she came home and married Grandpère."

"But what about him? The one she was seeing too much of?"

Isabelle looks at Jean-Paul. "I don't know, do you? She's never said."

"They can't have been really in love . . ." thinks Ulli aloud.

146

"Oh Ulli! 'Really in love!'" mocks Isabelle. "That wasn't what Grandmère was so worked up about, believe me. There's a lot you can do without being *really in love*. Still, as it turned out she had a great time in Vienna. She's still got friends there. What's it called, Jean-Paul? That stuff she makes?"

"Viennese milk bread."

"Oh yes, that's it. You'd like it, Ulli. It's great when it's hot. But it never tastes quite as good as you think it's going to be when you smell it baking. And it sticks to your teeth."

They are ruthless, Ulli knows, watching the brother and sister sprawled on her bed, so much at their ease, so watchful as they go over the story of how their grandmother separated their mother from an unsuitable lover. They would do the same for their own children, if the need arose. Lovingly, knowledgeably, surely. This is how they stay as they are.

Tomorrow Isabelle's mother will walk through the garden as she always does, with her head up and the tray in her hand, keeping everything in view. Her son, her garden, her land, her contacts in Paris who are all old friends she's known for ever. *Les amis de toujours.* She holds everything in place, effortlessly, so that everything prospers. Even the little Finnish girl, who may be turning out to be a bit of a mistake.

Ulli does not let herself dream of Jorma. Only one night sticks in her memory. His parents were away, and they were alone under the wooden sky of Jorma's bedroom. It was like having their own house. She climbed out of bed with Jorma watching her.

"Come back to bed."

"I can't, I'm starving."

She could have eaten up the house. She had never been so hungry.

Every evening, Isabelle's mother brings in some small special thing for her to eat. Olives and mozzarella cheese. Pumpernickel, because Ulli had once said they mostly ate black bread at home. A shiny black handful of Italian cherries. Ulli does her best, chopping the food up, pushing it around her plate to make it look less. But tonight she won't have to. Ulli is starving. Her mouth prickles with saliva at the thought of a golden-crusted hot new slice of bread, with pale Normandy butter oozing through it. No honey or jam, just the tastes of butter and the bread which Isabelle's mother has made. She'll swallow every mouthful, and run her licked finger round the plate to pick up the last crumbs.

In the forests of the north, given the time-change, Jorma will be asleep. There, it never really gets dark. The camp-fire will have died down to ash and trampled ground, and Jorma will be sleeping soundly after his day on the lake, in and out of the water teaching the children to swim, and to tack little one man dinghies across the bay. They are children who would never have a holiday at all, if it weren't for the charity funded by Jorma's parents and their friends, and the voluntary work done by the young people. As Jorma's mother says, "It's nice to be able to give something back."

Jorma won't dream, after his long day in the resinous air. It knocks out city-dwellers who aren't used to it. In his sleep he'll be alone, knowing he has done a good day's work. He used to laugh at his mother and her charities, but now he's beginning to understand that there is something in it after all. If we don't help, who will?

Emily's Ring

"It's still got the pattern on it. Even after it's been inside a fish."

"Let's see. Oh look, they're little hearts. All joined up. They should've put a photo in the paper."

"I don't reckon he even knew what a bass was, that young chap they sent to interview me. I could see him thinking, who's to say I didn't make it all up? Anyone can produce a ring and say they found it in a fish. But do you like it, love? It's yours if you want it."

"It's too small. It won't even go on my little finger."

"Maybe they had smaller fingers in those days. Bennet & Bonner's reckoned on this ring being more than a hundred years old."

"It's lovely though. Someone must've been sad to lose it."

I wish this wind would stop blowing. I am sure it makes Louise cry more, though Mama says she must be out in the air. Perhaps we shall have sun later. This morning Papa said the children must bathe today even if it rains, because that is why we have come. Dr Seton's orders are that all the children should bathe in the sea twice daily. But they are so thin after the whooping cough, and it rains and the waves rush in so fast. I am afraid that while I am watching one of them another will be knocked down.

"I have not brought you here to be idle, Emily," Mama said when I asked if we could wait until the weather was better before we started sea-bathing.

Perhaps it is a little warmer. There is no one else on the beach today, and I am glad of it because Papa wishes the children to bathe naked, and I know that many will think it indecent. They are happy now, all five of them burrowing in the sand, making a castle. And Louise in my lap, asleep at last.

"Look, Emily! We are going to put these shells on top."

"Very good, Alice."

She runs off, her cheeks whipped red by the wind. William and Henry are digging hard, hurling up sand behind them.

"Emily! Emily! Look at our moat!"

I wave and smile. Louise is heavy in my lap, and damp too. But at least she is not crying. Last night she would not stop screaming until I gave her laudanum drops. I was afraid she would wake Papa and Mama.

Margaret races across the sands and thumps down beside me.

"Hush! You will wake the baby."

Margaret does not like the baby. She is seven years old and she is tired of babies. I cannot blame her. There have been so many. William, Margaret, Alice, little Henry, then Paul, and now Louise. Margaret is seven, the same age as I was —

"Let me see your ring, Emily."

I draw it out from inside my bodice. It hangs around my neck on a piece of black silk ribbon. I never take it off. Once Papa said he would give me a silver chain to hang it upon, but Mama said that was foolish. "The ring is much too small for her. Why can she not give it to Margaret, or Alice?"

But Margaret and Alice knew better than to set up a cry for it. They looked at me with big eyes and said nothing. They know that my own mother gave me my ring when I was seven, the same age as Margaret. That was the year she died. I have often wondered if she knew she was going to die when she gave it to me. It fitted my finger perfectly. The next year, when I was eight, Papa married Mama. That is what I was told to call her the first time that I saw her, and now, even in my own head, I find I cannot stop calling her by that name.

Last night a gentleman complimented Papa upon his family as he walked on the promenade. I walked behind, holding Louise.

"A fine family, sir."

I believe he thought I was the nursemaid.

"Emily, Emily, please!"

"What is it, Margaret?"

"May I wear your ring? Just for a minute? I'll be careful, I promise I will."

I look down at her thin, eager face. I think of those nights when I held her upright while she choked and whooped. Often she was sick, and I would hold the bowl for her and wipe her face with lavender water afterwards. She is a good child, Margaret. She does not fuss.

"Very well, then," I say. "Give me your finger." I untie the ribbon, and take off my little silver ring. I slip it on to Margaret's lunger. "Careful, Margaret, it is loose. You are thinner since you had the whooping cough."

She turns the ring proudly so the little chased hearts catch the light. "It's beautiful, Emily."

"Yes."

But when I look up I see a strange figure kneeling by the children's sandcastle. A young man. He is digging hard with William's spade. I get up carefully, holding Louise, taking Margaret's hand.

"I hope the children are not troubling you, sir."

But he is only my age. Nearly a man, but mostly a boy, like William and Henry. His face is flushed like theirs. He is not embarrassed.

"We are to have battlements, and a drawbridge," he announces. "William! Where is the wood for the drawbridge?"

"There!" shouts William, and dashes to fetch a flat, white piece of driftwood. As he runs back the sun comes out behind him. He is not a boy any more, but a dark shape running out of the light. I smile, then I remember. They must bathe.

"Oh Emily, we want to finish our castle."

"Afterwards." I turn to the young man. "I am sorry. They are here for sea-bathing. They have all been unwell."

"Sea-bathing twice a day. I know all about that," he says.

It would be indelicate to ask if he has been ill too, but now I can see that he has. He is tall and angular and paler

153

than he should be. That is why he is so eager to build a castle with the children. He has been ill, and is bored and perhaps a little lonely.

And then Louise wakes. At once her face darkens and she opens her mouth and screams. Tiny red patches appear on her temples. I rock her but she only roars more loudly. How am I to bathe the children while Louise screams like this? Louise has perfect lungs and has never been ill in her life. All she suffers from is rage and teething.

"It is her teeth," I say, but Louise's shrieks drown my voice.

"How on earth will you bathe 'em all?"

"I shall stand on the edge and hold Paul."

"And the baby as well?"

"No, I find a place for her in the sand. I make a hollow so she does not roll away. It is enough for me to hold Paul and watch the others."

He whistles through his teeth. He is only a schoolboy, really. "Listen. Let me help you. I'd like to, awfully."

The children jump about, delighted.

"Oh no, really I cannot allow you to —" But Louise screams so loud I have a headache already. I bend down and place her on the sand. For a second she is silent, then, gathering breath, she howls again. I look down at her and think, "I shall leave you there. I am not going to carry you any more." But I know that I shall. How can I go home to Papa and Mama without Louise?

"I'll take the boys in for you. What do you say?" Already he is taking off his boots, peeling off his stockings. What an extraordinary young man. His feet are long and white and bony. I look away. William and Henry caper, stripping off their clothes and letting them fall on the sand. The wind blows, the sun shines on their thin white bodies. Even Paul is tugging at his boots. Alice and Margaret jump up and down, their petticoats flapping.

"Their papa," I stammer, "their papa wishes . . ." I am blushing. I clear my throat and begin again. "Their papa wishes them to bathe without their clothes. They do so by his express direction." I look hastily up and down the beach. No one is in sight, no one at all. No one to see the shocking sight of William and Henry dancing on the sands, Alice and Margaret tearing off their petticoats. I kneel down to take off little Paul's dress.

The young man's toes are sinking into the sand. "I'll stand in the shallows and duck 'em in for you, shall I?"

I smile and nod. William and Henry shriek with excitement and grab hold of his hands. Paul's clothing flies in my face. Louise will make herself sick with screaming if she does not stop soon. The sand and the sun are in my eyes and now Alice is yelling too.

"Emily! Emily!"

I turn my head, holding Paul still with one hand.

"Emily!"

She and Margaret have taken off their clothes already and are down by the edge of the water. What will the young man think of us? What will he say when he goes home? He will not understand Papa's views on hygiene. But there is no use thinking of that now. Bright waves rush in behind them, sparkling. The wind blows hard, tugging my bonnet. More sand blows into my eyes.

"What is it, Alice?"

"May we bathe too? Just here? Right at the edge?"

I struggle to hold on to Paul, who is trying to wriggle out of my grasp. Louise's cry has changed, it is high, desperate, sobbing. I must pick her up. And there they are, Alice and Margaret, dancing naked on the edge of the sea.

"Yes!" I call back. In the water at least they will be decent. "You may bathe! But not too far! Not too far in, Alice!" Margaret waves at me, a grave, delighted little flick of her hand, and both the little girls turn to the water.

And now Paul hurls himself on to the sand, raging because his sisters are in the water and he is not. And there go William and Henry too, walking off down the beach with the young man, finding the best place to go into the sea. I smile, thinking of how they will come back happy, and the young man will talk and perhaps tell me his name, even though it is not proper. I pick up Louise and wipe her red, tear-crusted cheeks. She will not stop crying. I pat her back, wrap her shawl more tightly around her. Sometimes that will calm her, but this time it makes no difference.

"Louise," I say, "Louise, Louise," but she is beyond hearing my voice. I think of what it must be like to be Louise, trapped in layers of prickling wool, wet and sore and screaming hour after hour. But it is better not to think of what babies' lives are like. I cannot rock her while she thrashes like a fish. I have never known a baby as angry as Louise. I think of the laudanum bottle. When I tip it up, one drop falls on Louise's horn spoon, then another. She sucks and bites the spoon. She will suck anything. She is greedy, Louise. And there is Paul on the sand, curled into a tight, furious ball. Paul cannot bear any of this. The sea is too big for him and his brothers can always do what he cannot.

"Paul, get up this instant." I bend down to him but he kicks and howls and will not let me near him. "Paul, I shall tell Papa." But he cannot hear me. He thuds his head against the sand, trying to hurt himself. He is purple. My head bangs with the noise of Paul and Louise and the wind, and I want to leave both of them there, to run away down the beach as far as I can where there are no children any more, only water. Somewhere out of the wind.

"Paul, please!" I begin, and then I hear Alice again. I turn. She is up to her knees in the water, a white twig against the bright bouncing waves. She is stiff, like a twig, pointing and screaming.

I do not know how I get to the water but I am there. Louise and Paul are behind me on the sand and I can hear nothing but the sea sucking and roaring round me. It is strong. It drags my skirts, pulls me as I struggle to keep upright. I seize hold of Alice. She is slippery, her wet hair streaming down her naked body. A wave catches her and she slides away through my hands, but I have her by the hair and as the sea fights to knock me down I haul Alice up.

"Alice! Alice! Where is Margaret!"

But Alice will not look at me. Her mouth is pressed so tight it is a single line in her face.

"Alice! Tell me! Where is Margaret? Where has she gone?"

I grasp Alice and I shake her, hard and then harder, but I cannot shake a sound out of her. The waves flash and tumble and shine like silver so I can see nothing. The sea surges round us and Alice stares at the bright bouncing waves while ice creeps up my neck and into my hair.

Swimming into the Millennium

Kirsty hands me the envelope and watches while I open it.

"Oh my God, Kirsty. What did this cost you?"

It's a three-month trial subscription to the Belvedere Hotel Health Club. I hold it like a chain letter that will bring death if you slight it. What am I going to do with it? These aren't my kind of places. I haven't got the right sort of trainers, even.

"You'll love it," says Kirsty. "They let me look round. It's like another world."

And I thank her, of course I do, over and over until she almost believes me. Because Kirsty isn't stupid, and a sister who's known you since you were born isn't the easiest person to deceive.

"I'll go tomorrow," I tell her.

"They give you a check-up," she says. "They work out a personal exercise programme for you."

"Great," I say. The word "personal" is one of my aversions. Personal loan. Personal hygiene. Personal safety. It's only a way of wrapping up the bad news that you're in debt, or dirty, or likely to be mugged. Or, in this case, about to be half-killed with weights and

159

exercise bikes in between showing off the size of your backside to a changing-room full of slender, leaping twenty-one-year-olds.

The Hotel Belvedere is very à la posh, as my nan used to say. Not old, comfortable posh, but new, matt-black, designer-dresses-on-the-waitresses posh. The rumour is that business isn't going too well. They have opened up the health club to non-residents, for a sum I don't want to know because it will make me feel too guilty. *Think of it as an early Christmas present,* Kirsty said. *You can get yourself into shape for the Millennium!*

They show me the gym, a jungle of black leather, metal implements, and tiny TV screens so you don't get bored while running on a treadmill or cycling to nowhere. Alex, who shows me round, takes it for granted that I want to be here. He's very professional, talking about personal-fitness targets and setting myself manageable goals. But he's friendly, in an American sort of way. We are on the way out, and I'm thinking, "At least I can tell Kirsty I've been," when suddenly Alex said, "And of course you have full use of the hotel pool as part of your membership."

"Could I see it?" I ask, dropping the idea of asking him what partial use of the pool might entail.

"Of course." He sweeps ahead, pressing lift buttons, holding doors for me, allowing me to admire the way the muscles bulge in his calves. Isn't it strange how the best-developed specimens of humanity tend to look the least human?

And then, between one breath and the next, I fall in love. Alex moves aside so I can see better, and there it is.

Sleek, still, blue water in a frame of dark-blue tiles. Beyond, a mass of plants in long troughs, then windows that curve inwards as if we are on a ship, then the city five floors below. There are sun-loungers at one end, with thick dark-blue cushions. There's a blue smell, too, like the sea.

"Can you really sunbathe?"

"Sure. It's a real sun-trap up here."

And the walls are the colour of summer skies, without a cloud on them. There's nobody here at all. No kids bombing each other off the side. No fit young men blowing their noses into the water after twenty lengths of crawl. No chalkboard saying the pool is reserved for school use from 9 a.m. to 3.30 p.m.

"Is it always like this?"

"Like what?"

"So quiet."

"Yeah, I guess so."

If Alex wasn't here I'd jump in and swim in my bra and knickers, but he's not going to leave me alone. He's itching to get back to the gym. I look back over my shoulder as we leave, and the water seems to rock a little, as if it's impatient, too.

I go out and buy a new swimsuit. It's black and expensive and it lets you move any way you want in the water. My daughter Nicky pounces into the bag and shakes out the swimsuit, ready to scorn it until she sees the price tag.

"Mu-um!"

"It's my Millennium present to myself."

And that sets her off. Walkman, new top she's seen in Next — or maybe she'll just have the money and go on the school skiing trip after all . . . I say nothing. I'm upstairs, wrapping my swimsuit in a towel, finding a clip to pin up my hair.

Nobody stops me as I enter the hotel. I sign in at the front desk, and take the lift to the fifth floor. I wish I'd bought a sports bag. I look everything I am, a forty-five-year-old overweight mum with her stuff crammed into a recyclable Tesco bag. But as I go along the corridor to the pool, I smell the blue smell again. It makes me think of towels hanging over verandah railings, and our cold bare feet on bare boards, and the sea settling into summer darkness. We always had our windows open, and we could hear the sea on the quietest nights.

I open the door to the pool. I hear a splash, a voice flying up to the high ceiling, a laugh. The pool is broken up into blue squares, shivering with light. There's a boy in the water, on his back, backstroking, laughing up at another boy who kneels on the side.

They're not boys, they're young men. Early twenties perhaps. Playing and laughing as if the pool belongs to them. Which it does. I am about to slip back into the fluorescent corridor with my dry swimming things when the one kneeling by the pool looks up and sees me. He smiles at me, quickly, apologetically, as if he knows that it won't take anything to send me away for ever.

"I am sorry we are noisy," he says. "Only there was no one else here — usually we are very quiet."

He speaks English beautifully. He's dark and neat and there are little drops of water shining all over his body, as if he's only just this minute come out of the pool. The boy in the water rolls over and treads water, flicking back his hair. Then he ducks down and comes up streaming. He's big and powerful, a bit younger than the other, with heavy white shoulders.

"We are training," says the boy on the side.

"Oh, I see." I don't see. I see that they are both young and beautiful and they belong here, but for some reason they don't mind that I've come and they aren't alone any more. They're quite easy with it, and so I feel easy too, as I walk down the side of the pool towards the ladies' changing-room. I take off my clothes in the long room with its floor-length mirrors, and I walk naked to the shower without caring and I soap myself with the blue seaweed scrub and let the water run all over my face and hair so I'll be clean before I go into the pool. I think of Nicky and Jack and Elinor when they were little, racing about dragging towels on the floor and needing to pee and screeching when I dried their hair. I shut my eyes luxuriously and let the water roll down my breasts. Then I put on the new swimsuit and it fits perfectly. I look big in the mirrors, but I don't look wrong.

When I come out they are both going down the pool, side by side, swimming a smooth, strong front crawl that hardly makes a splash except when they come to the end and turn underwater, leaving a crowd of bubbles behind them. I climb down the steps at the shallow end, lean forward, and strike out in a choppy breaststroke. It feels like a long time since I've been swimming. But the water closes round me and I begin to relax. All the lists float out of my mind: order the turkey by the first week in

December, sign Jack's consent form for hockey camp, Christmas-card list, present list, food list, things-to-do list. And then the second list that's been nagging at me for the whole year: the Millennium list. A thousand ways of wrapping up a thousand years, and I'm not tempted by any of them.

The lists float out of my mind, and the water takes them away. I count strokes, count lengths, hear the puff and snort of my breath. I'm concentrating so hard that I don't notice for a while that the dark boy is at my side of the pool now, watching me. When I do, I stop swimming and stand shoulder-deep in the water.

"Hello," he says. "I am watching your strokes."

"I noticed."

"You are working too hard. You must make it easy for yourself."

The next minute he's vaulted off the side and he's beside me in the water. "Here. You must relax your shoulders. When you go forward, keep your body in a line. You will use your glide. Now, you are kicking against yourself. I'll show you."

He shows me. I try again. Suddenly it's there: less effort, more energy. I surge forward.

"Good. But your head is still too high. You must lie in the water, not on it."

The other boy is still going up and down the pool, as if swimming is no more to him than breathing.

"He's Eugene. I am Evrus. Easy to remember!"

"And I'm Frances. What are you training for?"

Evrus smiles. "We are swimming into the Millennium."

"What does that mean?"

"You know the Millennium. You cannot escape it. You have to have a celebration or else you are a criminal — you know this? Some people are drinking into it. Some people are partying into it. Some people are climbing into their beds and pulling the sheets over their heads. We are swimming into the Millennium, and this is our training. We come every day. We are friends. We like to be together."

He smiles at me, that clear smile I haven't seen on my own children's faces since they turned thirteen.

"We love each other," he says. "You know what that means?"

"Yes. I know what that means."

The words stir inside me like moths which have been shut up in a cupboard winter after winter, struggling to spread their wings. I am afraid he'll see too much in my face, so I scoop up a handful of water and pour it over myself.

"Thanks for the help with my breaststroke," I say, and I plunge back into the water, letting it cover me.

But that's not the end. They are there the next time I go to the pool, and the next. I am going every day now. I don't know the price of clementines at Marks & Spencer. I haven't found the right cardigan for my ex-mother-in-law. We'll be having the last frozen turkey I can grab off the shelf, this year. Evrus times us against the big clock on the wall. Eugene is shaving seconds off his four-hundred metres. Evrus himself dives into the deepest water, hardly parting it, and swims underwater so far we are afraid his lungs are bursting. I catch

Eugene's eye when Evrus finally comes up, and we both grin in relief. I stay at the pool for half an hour, perhaps. I can't take more. I know they'll spend an hour, two hours, even three. Time doesn't matter to them. They are young, they are beautiful, and Evrus has money, somehow. It's the first of December, the fifth, the twelfth. Christmas rolls away from my mind, like a striped and sparkling burden. Television is going crazy with the longest party in the world. People in the streets look almost frightened, as if they know they're about to fail and it'll be just another night, not magical or brilliant or different at all. Only a few days to go now.

"You're coming on," says Eugene. "You're doing great."

But it's Evrus who coaches me. I am a forty-five year-old woman, big and sleek, with moths flying inside her and opening their wings. December sunlight comes through the skylight in the changing-room and makes patterns on my bare flesh. I know it's winter, but it feels warm. I can swim thirty lengths now, easily. I don't pant and gasp for breath anymore. I lean forward and let the water take me. Evrus has taught me how to breathe.

The pool will be open on December 31st. It never closes. Evrus has checked; Eugene has double-checked. They'll be here at ten p.m. They'll be poised, one at each end of the pool, leaning forward. When the second hand sweeps round to the top they'll launch themselves out into the water. They won't stop swimming, whatever happens, until the clocks strike for midnight all over the city. I think of midnight flying around the globe, with the chimes of all the churches chasing it.

"You come too, Frances," says Evrus, resting his head against Eugene's shoulder. "You must be here for midnight."

"Yes," I say. The children will be out, of course. "See you next millennium, Mum!" they'll say, laughing.

"Yes," I say again. "I'll come. As long as I won't be in your way."

But I know I won't be. They have everything, all the hours of the present and all the hours to come. They have so much that it spills over on to me.

And now it's half an hour to midnight. The water feels dark and velvety, midnight blue. For a while I watch the flash of Eugene's arms, the fume of bubbles that trails after Evrus. Then I close my eyes and I swim forward, into the Millennium.

Lisette

This is an old story, which my grandfather first told me when I was about the same age as Lisette.

My grandfather travelled a great deal before the war, in Europe, in South America, and in the East. He spoke French, German, Spanish, and a little Russian. Languages lighted on him effortlessly, and he grew impatient when he saw me struggling over French homework. I remember the way he scored through my crab-like Cyrillic script, when I began to learn Russian.

"It's not a code, they're words. Look." And he wrote out the text for me again. The words flowed from his pen as surely as a letter to a friend.

He travelled on business. My grandfather was an engineer who worked in the export of machine tools, and this is how he met Lisette's parents, before she was born. He was in Paris, negotiating a deal with a large family firm. A lunch was arranged. The managing director was about sixty, much older than my grandfather, and in the process of handing over to his second son, Claude. Claude was supposed to be handling this deal, but the father couldn't quite leave things alone. At the lunch he fussed over the wines as if he were the host. My grandfather was tired, anyway, and beginning to feel unwell. He never enjoyed these long lunches, bred of business, slurring over into private life. He struggled to eat the exceptionally good *caneton aux navets*. Halfway through the meal he was struck by an excruciating pain in his chest and left shoulder. He couldn't conceal it: he had to close his eyes and sit perfectly still while the pain passed. But it wouldn't pass. Claude had noticed by now, and so had his father.

"Are you all right? What is it?"

They'd done business two or three times now. They weren't friends, but they were cordial acquaintances, and their faces showed genuine concern.

"Just a pain," said my grandfather. "It's nothing."

But the pain still wouldn't pass. Claude rose from the table and went to the telephone. "We'll go straight to my brother's," he said when he returned.

"My elder son," explained old M. Beck, "is a doctor."

He said this almost apologetically. Very soon the car arrived, and old M. Beck went with my grandfather while Claude remained to preside over the meal.

It wasn't far. Daniel Beck had an apartment and consulting-room in Montparnasse, near the Coupole. He was expecting my grandfather, and he examined him very thoroughly. My grandfather said Daniel Beck was one of those rare doctors who immediately make you feel confident. Whatever the problem is, they are on your side, vigilant, ready to defeat it. Daniel listened carefully to my grandfather's heart, took his pulse, asked a great many questions. In the end he said that he was almost certain it was nothing but a severe attack of heartburn. But, as a precaution, my grandfather should rest in his apartment for an hour, and then he would examine him again.

It was an act of real friendship, my grandfather explained to me. French people rarely open their homes to business acquaintances: they prefer to meet in restaurants. "He could easily have asked me to rest in his consulting-room."

But they went through the double doors into the hall, and into the *salon* where Daniel's wife, Lucie, was sitting on a sofa with her feet up, reading. She put down her book and half-rose as the men came in, and my grandfather saw that she was heavily pregnant.

"You'll have to excuse me," she said, grimacing at her own clumsiness as she fell back against the cushions. Lucie was a very small, slight woman, and the pregnancy looked enormous on her, like a distortion. Daniel explained the situation. Lucie was about to ring for some tea, because my grandfather was English, but Daniel said that Vichy water would be better.

My grandfather was very taken with them both. He opened up to Daniel's quick kindness, and the intelligence that shone from Lucie's face. They made him feel at home, he said. The place was full of books, and there were big vases of yellow tulips on the tables and in the fireplace. It was a large, quiet room, facing south.

"I'll leave you for a while. I'm in the consulting-room if there's any difficulty, Lucie. The best thing would be for you both to have a little sleep."

But of course they didn't sleep. My grandfather was beginning to feel better, and the pleasure of being in a family home after weeks of hotels made him more talkative than usual. Lucie was bored, and glad of his company.

"I have to rest quite a lot," she said. Her eyes were stained with shadow, and she didn't look well. My grandmother was a tall, strong woman who barely sat down throughout her pregnancies, and my grandfather was strangely touched by Lucie's fragility.

"Lucie was very independent," he said. "You could tell that immediately. But she would always be the kind of woman whom men want to protect."

While they were talking, it emerged that this was not Lucie's first child. They had had a son the year before, who had been stillborn.

"It's why I rest every afternoon," said Lucie. "Sometimes I wonder if I did too much last time, but Daniel says it would have made no difference."

The flowers shone as the sun moved round. My grandfather was warm, dozy, at peace in the relief after pain. He had nothing to do but wait until Daniel came back. Sometimes he and Lucie talked, sometimes they fell silent. When Daniel opened the door to the *salon*, my grandfather wasn't even sure if he'd been asleep or awake.

There was nothing really wrong, Daniel concluded, but he advised my grandfather on some changes of diet. They talked a little more, exchanged addresses, and my grandfather went back to the hotel in a taxi.

Daniel, of course, should have inherited the business. But he chose medicine, and worse than that, he chose to specialize in the treatment of tuberculosis among the urban poor. By the time my grandfather met him, he was

171

setting up a new clinic in Paris, which was connected to a sanatorium in the Alps. The sanatorium was supported by a charitable foundation, but new funding for the clinic was badly needed. Daniel saw many more patients than he was able to treat effectively. Lucie was involved in the fund-raising, but she hadn't been able to do much over the past year or so.

My grandfather saw them again, the next time he went to Paris, and the next. He organized a donation to the clinic from his firm, which was glad to show goodwill towards valuable clients. They didn't know that old M. Beck disapproved of Daniel's work. My grandfather also made donations of his own. He never visited the clinic, because he had a horror of TB, but he was always eager to hear how things were going. He found it hard to believe, at first, that Daniel and Lucie felt no such horror. He was baffled, then moved by their passionate interest in the disease. For years, Lucie and Daniel had spent three months at the sanatorium each summer. Lucie worried about the isolation of the patients. Some of them were in the sanatorium for as much as two years. She told my grandfather about her efforts to put on concerts and plays, and to establish a fund to enable families to visit their sick relations.

"They've got to have some life in there, otherwise it's like a prison!"

Things went well. In the July of the year my father met Daniel and Lucie, Lisette was born. He saw her first at five months, then again at a year. He was doing a great deal of business with Claude Beck. Lisette was rather like her mother, and not a strong baby. She battled her way through bronchitis, which narrowly escaped becoming pneumonia. If it hadn't been for Lucie's nursing, she might not have survived.

"You have to remember that this was before antibiotics," my grandfather said. He remembers how light Lisette was when he was given her to hold, with her spidery little hand clutching the fold of her shawl. She had big dark eyes, and a quiff of dark hair. My grandfather was fascinated by her difference from his own bouncing, rosy babies.

"She was tough, though, in her way," he said. "She had to be, to keep going. There was a real character there, right from the beginning."

I felt a little jealous of Lisette, when he said that, and wondered if I had a real character.

Daniel and Lucie thought Lisette was an astonishing baby. She could speak before she could walk. By the time she was eighteen months she knew a dozen songs. It seemed that there was no question of another child, but that didn't worry Lucie and Daniel, as far as my grandfather could tell. Lisette was enough for them.

"She was quite a serious little thing," my grandfather said. "She didn't run about and scream, the way children do. But she was happy. Lucie always had the double doors open, between the *salon* and the nursery, so Lisette could go in and out. When she was playing in there, we would hear her laughing to herself. I remember when we took her on the carousel for the first time, in the park. Lucie thought she might be afraid, because she wasn't very bold, but when Lisette came around on her little horse she was laughing to herself and patting the horse as if it was alive. She would have been pretending something. She was always pretending something."

I could tell that he had been very fond of Lisette.

When the war came, my grandfather was too old to fight, and my father was still too young. The machine-tool factory switched to manufacturing tools for aeroplane production. "We were so far behind the Germans. People have no idea how far behind we were. And it had been obvious for years what was going to happen. We nearly lost the war, never forget that."

My grandfather travelled often in Germany. "It isn't true that people didn't know what was going on. Everyone knew. You'd go into negotiation and ask after Herr Baumann or Herr Goldmann, whom you'd dealt with last time, and they would say he had moved, or been transferred. But everyone knew."

Daniel and Lucie never thought of leaving Paris, as far as my grandfather knew. They were Parisians through and through, and then there was the clinic. Besides, the fall of France happened so quickly that it would have taken someone very much more worldly than Daniel to read the signs, get the documents, and get out. Even Claude, the epitome of the practical man, remained at his managing director's desk in his factory. By now he had formally succeeded his father.

But Claude did survive. He was indeed a practical man, and a shrewd one, with a streak of daring no one would have guessed from watching him swallow his *caneton aux navets* while finicking over the last clause of a deal. He got his family out through Spain and Portugal, but to everyone's astonishment he went to

London for training, and returned to France to work undercover for the Resistance.

"He was certainly a highly intelligent man," my grandfather would say, a little ruminatively, still surprised after all these years by Claude. "He joined the Resistance. Yes, I know that *everyone* joined the Resistance, in retrospect, but Claude actually did."

Claude saw Daniel and Lucie once, when he was in Paris. He came without warning, for half an hour, to tell them he had a chance of getting them away, if they left immediately. Jews were being rounded up every day now. Jewish orphanages and old people's homes were being emptied. When Claude spoke to my grandfather, years later, he said that he had tried to persuade Daniel and Lucie to leave at once. It was very dangerous, because they would be travelling with a child, and the papers weren't good. But at least that way they would have a chance.

They wouldn't go. It was winter, and Lisette was ill. She had bronchitis again, not as badly as before, but pretty bad. Lucie was up all night with the bronchitis kettle. Lisette was underweight, and she had very little resistance. Daniel had got hold of a little oil stove, and some oil, but it was very cold in the apartment. They hardly ever went out. People were being picked up in the streets all the time. A mother would leave her children to buy bread, and she would never return.

"Lisette would not survive the journey," Daniel said, and Claude had to accept that Daniel knew best. He was, after all, the doctor. Claude had very little time left, and

175

he had to go. He didn't say goodbye to Lisette, because she was asleep.

Claude said it was strange to go into that apartment, after the fear of the streets. "You can't imagine what it was like in Paris then." But inside the apartment which my grandfather knew so well, the atmosphere was not at all as you would expect. Lucie and Daniel didn't seem anxious, or frightened, except for Lisette's health. Lucie sat with Lisette curled up in her lap, singing songs to her, both of them tucked under a quilt so that Lucie's body heat could keep Lisette warm. That was all they were thinking about. The next drink for Lisette, the next taking of her temperature, her cough, her breathing. Daniel no longer went to the clinic. As a Jewish doctor, he had been dismissed some time ago. He did see patients, and they would give him lard, or maybe a bag of flour, in exchange for his advice and whatever drugs he had left. Lisette never left the apartment.

"It was as if they thought if she was never seen, her existence could not be proved," said Claude. "But of course they had all the records and papers. No one was invisible."

It was about a month later that Daniel, Lucie and Lisette were taken. Claude found out a certain amount of what happened to them. Daniel and Lucie were separated immediately, but Lisette stayed with her mother. A woman from the next apartment block saw them at Drancy, still together.

Lucie died at Auschwitz. Whether Lisette was still with her, I don't know. My mind halts at the thought of their separation, but very probably it happened.

When I think of Lisette then, I think of a brief passage of film which was taken by some camp official at Auschwitz, for the records. I think of him standing there, wielding his ciné-camera.

The film shows the arrival of a train. It only lasts for a few seconds, fifteen, perhaps. A small child is lifted down from a cattle-car, on to a ramp. She is about four, some years younger than Lisette, who would have been eight when she died. But Lisette was always small for her age. This child is as round as a football. Her parents have wrapped her in layers and layers of clothing, everything she possesses.

"At least we can make sure she won't be cold."

She wears a thick scarf wrapped around her head. From it her face stares out, pale, bewildered, recognizing nothing. She looks from side to side. She does not cry. The film ends.

This isn't my story. It isn't even my grandfather's story, although I heard it from him. But I felt I had to tell it, even if you're tired of it, even if you've heard it all before.

ISIS publish a wide range of books in large print, from fiction to biography. A full list of titles is available free of charge from the address below. Alternatively, contact your local library for details of their collection of ISIS large print books.

Details of ISIS complete and unabridged audio books are also available.

Any suggestions for books you would like to see in large print or audio are always welcome.

7 Centremead
Osney Mead
Oxford OX2 0ES
(01865) 250333